Rikki guided the twins into their bedroom and closed the door.

An hour later, she, Meg and Emma had all made new jewelry, which they then wore for a special tea party, and she'd read three books to the girls while they cuddled up on the bed.

Rikki snuggled with them, content. They smelled like bubble bath. A strange feeling wrapped around her until she thought she might cry. These precious little girls, so eager for female attention, had brought her a new kind of happiness. It reinforced her dream of having a big family. The more the merrier. No child left behind, all loved equally.

Basically, it was a no-brainer.

She'd made her decision.

Dear Reader

I am absolutely thrilled to have a January release in the year Mills & Boon celebrates its 100th birthday. Never in my wildest dreams did I see myself as one of their authors when I first started out writing romance in 2000.

I would never have discovered the wonderful world of Medical™ Romance had it not been for Mills & Boon. I know when I open one of their romance books I am assured of quality, drama, and an upbeat ending. With so much sadness in the world, I need my frequent romance fix, and always know where to find it—right here at my favourite publisher, Mills & Boon.

Now I'd like to tell you a bit about my new book, SINGLE DAD, NURSE BRIDE. I don't know about you, but nothing gets to me more than to see a father with his children. Now, that *is* sexy! When I see grown men bend down to tend to the needs of their small children, I get all gooey inside. Nothing could be tenderer. In my story, I've chosen a suitable match for my overwhelmed single dad. An unselfish, though emotionally imperfect nurse shows him the true meaning of giving, helps him learn to be a better father, and manages to steal his heart in the process.

Happy 100th Birthday, Mills & Boon, and thank you for all you've done to boost romance in our lives!

Best wishes and happy reading

Lynne Marshall

SINGLE DAD, NURSE BRIDE

BY
LYNNE MARSHALL

MILLS & BOON

Pure reading pleasure™

First published in Great Britain 2007
Large Print edition 2008
Harlequin Mills & Boon Limited,
Eton House, 18-24 Paradise Road,
Richmond, Surrey TW9 1SR

© Janet Maarschalk 2007

ISBN: 978 0 263 19966 6

Set in Times Roman 16½ on 18¼ pt.
17-0708-48998

Printed and bound in Great Britain
by Antony Rowe Ltd, Chippenham, Wiltshire

BACHELOR DADS
Single Doctor… Single Father!

At work they are skilled medical professionals, but at home, as soon as they walk in the door, these eligible bachelors are on full-time fatherhood duty!

These devoted dads
still find room in their lives for love…

It takes very special women to win the hearts of these dedicated doctors, and a very special kind of caring to make these single fathers full-time husbands!

Lynne Marshall has been a registered nurse in a large hospital in California for over twenty years. Currently she is an advice/triage nurse for fifteen internal medicine doctors. She began writing in 2000, and has earned over a dozen contest awards since. She is happily married to a police lieutenant, and has a grown daughter and son. Besides her passion for writing Medical™ Romance stories, she loves travel, reading, and power walks.

Recent titles by the same author:

IN HIS ANGEL'S ARMS
HER L.A. KNIGHT
HER BABY'S SECRET FATHER

CHAPTER ONE

THE hair on Rikki Johansen's neck prickled. She chalked it up to internal radar as she always *knew* when a certain doctor came to the orthopedic ward. The fact she had a teeny tiny crush on him was beside the point.

Dr. Dane Hendricks didn't look pleased, and the scowl on his face proved something was wrong. His agitated demeanor flashed a warning, and made her wish she could hide. With his broad shoulders squared, and an IV piggyback in his hand, his intense green eyes scanned the nurses' station for a victim. He hadn't spotted her yet. She ducked her head.

"Which nurse is taking care of room 416?"

Rikki had just started her shift that Thursday morning, and couldn't avoid him. She glanced at her clipboard. Yep, she was the lucky nurse about to get chewed out. Dr. Henricks's no-nonsense glare made her wish she could swap patient assignments with someone…anyone.

"Over here." She nonchalantly raised her hand and pretended to be distracted by more important business, thumbing through a chart. She leaned back in her chair. She was damned if she'd let him know how much he and his demanding, perfectionist ways scared her.

His long strides echoed off the linoleum. Each step closer brought a twinge of dread. Rikki clenched her jaw, preparing for the worst.

He shoved the empty secondary IV under her gaze. "Whose name is that?"

"James Porter?" she read from the small plastic bag. Had she passed the test? She glanced upward into his dead-serious eyes, trying her hardest not to blink.

"Correct. So why did I find this hanging on, Patrick Slausen's IV?"

Uh-oh. She jumped up from her seat, and almost bumped into his chest. He stepped back, training his no-nonsense stare on her.

At 7:15 a.m., not about to start making excuses

about how she'd just come on duty and hadn't assessed her patients in room 416 yet, she opted to keep things short and to the point.

"I'll see to this immediately, sir, and write an incident report. Did you notice any adverse reaction from the patient?"

His glower sent a shiver down her spine. She tensed, waiting for the worst.

He adjusted his trendy glasses. "Lucky for you, he's fine." He turned. "I'm going to have a little conversation with your supervisor while you check things out," he said over his shoulder, digging his heels into the lime-tinted floor.

Great. Two months on the job at Los Angeles Mercy Hospital, not even off probation yet, and he was going to complain to her boss about her. What did it matter that it wasn't her fault? She was damned if she'd grovel to the self-assured orthopedic surgeon. She knew how to take a setback. Hell, her whole life had been one challenge after another. He wouldn't get her down.

Not today.

Not tomorrow. That is, if she still had her job tomorrow.

At least the patient was OK. It could be worse.

Though rare, medication errors did happen in hospitals, and as an RN it was her job to see that they didn't. But no one was perfect, and nurses needed to feel it was safe to come forward and admit when they'd made mistakes without losing their jobs. The right thing to do was to immediately report the error to the nursing supervisor, fill out an incident report, and notify the patient's MD. This time Dr. Hendricks had beaten the nursing staff to the task. The outgoing nurse could not have noticed what she'd done. No one did something like this on purpose.

The best line of defense was always to check and double-check medications with the med sheet. Never rush. Allergic reactions from wrong medications could be fatal. Rikki knew that as well as she did her own shoe size.

What had they drummed into her head in nursing school? Check for the right patient, the right drug, the right dose, the right time, the right route, and then do it all again, and again, before giving a patient anything. Obviously the night nurse had been distracted, but that was still no excuse.

Rikki rushed into 416A, to Mr. Slausen, a total hip replacement, and began her head-to-toe assessment while taking vital signs.

"Good morning, gentlemen," she said to both patients. "Get any sleep last night?"

They both grumbled from their day-old whiskered faces something about how the night nurses never left them alone. If she hadn't been so distracted, she'd have teased them to brighten up their day, like she usually did with her patients. *Oh, come on. Those poor night nurses get bored. They have to keep waking you up to give them something to do.* But making a joke was the last thing on her mind this morning.

She noted on the chart that patient Slausen's antibiotic was to be given every six hours. The last dose had been given one hour before her shift had begun. Thank heavens James Porter, his roommate in bed B, was on the same dose of antibiotic for his below-the-knee amputation. The error had been the right drug, the right route, the right time, and the right dose, but the *wrong* patient. A careless mistake. And there was no antibiotic hanging for Mr. Porter, which meant he'd missed a dose. Not acceptable.

She handed Mr. Slausen his bedside Inspirometer after listening to his breath sounds. "Here you go. Deep breathe. See how far you can raise the balls." He'd sounded a little too quiet in his left lung. "Try for the smiley face area. We've got to re-expand your lungs."

She glanced at Mr. Porter, watching and waiting for his turn for vital signs. "Do yours, too. It's very important after surgery." He reluctantly reached for the plastic contraption that bore a silly happy face that elevated to various levels with each deep inhalation. She knew it might be uncomfortable for a post-op patient to do, but it lessened the chance of pneumonia.

Rikki didn't let on anything was wrong but, in her opinion, Dr. Hendricks had every right to be upset.

Janetta Gleason sat quietly while Rikki explained the mix-up with the medicine and the patients. She'd quickly learned she had a friend in her supervisor. Fair and just, Ms. Gleason never jumped to conclusions. The silver-and-black-haired lady smiled with kind gray eyes from behind her cluttered desk. Rikki bet she'd worn that same close-cropped tight Afro hairdo since the 1970s.

"I told Dane...I mean Dr. Hendricks...it wasn't your fault. I told him I'd talk to Rita from nights."

Rikki relaxed and studied a wall filled with pictures of the woman's young grandchildren and thought how one day she wanted to have several children of her own.

"Thanks. I'm not sure he likes new nurses, and that mix-up didn't help matters."

"Yes, well, he does like things just so." She rolled her eyes. "In a perfect world...maybe..."

Rikki handed the incident report across the computer. As she'd listed Dr. Dane Hendricks as first to notice the error, he'd have to sign it. She hoped Janetta would take it to him so she wouldn't have to face him again.

She had her hands full with a fresh hip replacement. Not to mention teaching Mr. Porter and his family how to care for his amputation stump in order to get him fitted for a prosthesis. Then across the hall she had the lady in traction with a fractured pelvis—a very demanding patient who was constantly on the call light. Thank goodness her roommate was more reasonable to deal with. Though that patient's compound fracture of the femur with metal rod placement looked much worse. It resembled Frankenstein's head, with hardware and screws protruding from the flesh, but suspended with traction in a lamb's-wool-lined canvas sling. Not a pretty sight.

The only thing she had to look forward to today was the first-of-the month party in the nursing lounge where they celebrated for anyone who had a birthday. November was her month, and on Saturday she'd turn twenty-six. Being raised in the foster-care system, special days like birthdays sometimes got overlooked. Today at work it was a given, her name was on the cake. For some dumb reason it made her happy.

Janetta read the incident report thoroughly and nodded her head in approval. "I'll pass this information on to Dane and counsel Rita."

"Thank you. Dr. Hendricks is the last person I want to see again today."

"He's actually a very nice man. He's been through a lot the last few years."

"Oh." That had never occurred to her. Hadn't she cornered the market on challenges?

"How are things going with your foster-kid?"

"Brenden is doing great. Thanks for asking. How about you? Have you signed on to replace that empty nest you're sitting on?"

"Actually, I've attended all of the training classes. They assessed my home, made sure I had appropriate space and childcare arrangements, and issued me a license. So I'm good."

"Great. I'll see you in the childcare center soon, then."

"Right. Hey, wasn't it you who transferred here because of our family care center?" Janetta asked, while she nonchalantly signed the paperwork.

Rikki nodded. "Yes. That and the fact Mercy pays better, so I could afford my two-bedroom apartment and still have two dimes to rub together at the end of the month. And the child-care center has been a godsend with Brenden."

"We've always been progressive here, so we finally had to listen to our working mothers."

"Absolutely."

"I only wish they'd had it when I was raising my kids."

"Yeah, but someone had to be the trailblazers."

Janetta laughed. Her smile brightened her eyes. "And I'll finally get to take advantage of it when I start foster-parenting."

"See? There is justice in the world."

Janetta's face grew solemn. Her gaze drifted somewhere deep within as if remembering something special. "Since Jackson died, I just feel like I need to give more back to the community." She forced another smile. "You seem to do a lot of that."

"Nah. But every little bit helps."

"And I commend you for volunteering."

"What goes around comes around. You know?"

"Karma?"

"More like the golden rule—do unto others…"

"Whatever your reasons, I'm impressed. Now, get back to work," Janetta said with a kind smile and a swish of her hand. "And don't forget to have some cake, girl!"

Dane knew what he had to do. He stripped off his specially made prescription OR goggles and placed them in the sterilization bin. He removed his blue paper cap, mask, and gown, and disposed of them.

An apology was in order.

He scrubbed his hands and threw some water on his face. After standing for three hours during surgery, he needed to shake out his legs. The nursing supervisor, Janetta Gleason, had explained the circumstances of his patient's medication error, and he'd realized he'd accused the wrong nurse.

Emma had had another upset tummy last night, and he'd spent two hours pacing with her in his arms. He knew the girls missed their mother, yet they never talked about her. Instead, they'd take turns with odd little ailments or aches that only a good long hug could cure. Unfortunately for him, too often it was in the middle of the night before his scheduled surgery days.

He loved holding their little sparrow-like bodies—so fragile and innocent. They were the best things to have ever happened to him, and since their birth four years ago, medicine had run a distant second on the priority scale.

He shook his head. Normally, he'd check out his data before leveling a full-on attack at a colleague, but he'd been tired and irritable, and then, damn, he'd found the wrong patient's medicine on his other patient's IV. Was it too much to ask for proper patient care? He'd jumped to conclusions and blasted the wrong nurse as a result. Well, he couldn't let his mistake lie. He slipped on a white coat over his scrubs.

Rikki. Yeah, that was her name.

He and the enchanting little nurse had made eye contact on several occasions on the hospital ward. She'd always offered a friendly though shy smile. He liked her huge brown eyes and glossy, butterscotch-colored hair. Not that he'd spent a lot of time noticing or anything, but she had an enticing piercing—a tiny diamond chip or crystal or something that looked like a sparkly, sexy mole just above her lip. At first he'd thought it was a fake stick-on thing, but over time he'd realized it was always in the same place.

It made him wonder what it would be like to kiss her. Would he feel it if he pressed his lips to her soft, sexy mouth? What was that about? He'd been too busy to ask anyone out on a date for months, let alone make out. Why think about it now?

He threw more water on his face and headed out the door. *I've been working too damn much.*

As soon as he wrote the post-op orders and notified the surgical patient's family that the knee replacement had been a success, he'd go back to the fourth floor and seek Rikki out. He owed it her to make things right.

Dane glanced at his watch. Too late. She'd already be off duty and he needed to pick up his daughters from childcare and take them for dinner at Grandma's. His apology would have to wait until tomorrow.

Rikki rushed into the blood donor center at Mercy Hospital. She'd promised to donate platelets tonight, a two-hour process, and the lab closed at 7:30 p.m. The teenager from next door, who she occasionally used as a babysitter, had arrived late.

She'd been hydrating herself and taking extra calcium and iron for the last week. She'd avoided analgesics that thinned the blood as a side effect. She knew the hospital's oncology department was always in need of the blood component that played an important role in blood coagulation. Without platelets, many patients wouldn't be able to survive chemotherapy or emergency surgeries.

She'd donated platelets during the first week of her employment when she had been going through orientation and they'd mentioned there was always a shortage in pediatric oncology. Having waited the required fifty-six days, she was ready to donate again, deciding to make it a routine.

Do unto others…her favorite foster-mother had always said.

After filling out the paperwork and being grilled about her sexual history—practically non-existent, thank you very much—she scooted back into the large over-stuffed lounger. She prepared to watch a movie on her one birthday splurge, a portable DVD player, while the nurse started the process.

She knew the drill. Her blood would be collected from one arm, sent through the platelet-phoresis machine where the platelets would be removed, and her own blood would be returned to her other arm. She recalled a weird feeling that made her flush all over and gave her a strange metallic taste in her mouth the last time she'd donated. The nurse had told her it was the anti-coagulant they used in the machine.

To help pass the time during the long donation that night, she'd chosen her kindest foster-mother's favorite movie, *Monty Python's Holy Grail*. A classic. She knew it was silly, but the two of them had always gotten such a kick out of the film when she was a young teenager. And laughing was good for the soul, the sweet Mrs. Greenspaugh had always said. After a long string of not-so-great foster-homes, she'd finally gotten a break with a terrific older lady. It had come at a perfect time in her life, too. Adele

Greenspaugh had taught her to appreciate her individuality, and to love herself.

Unfortunately, she'd died and Rikki had gotten sent to the worst home of her life when she'd been sixteen. All the confidence Mrs. Greenspaugh had built up the "do-good witch" she'd been sent to had torn down. Well, she hadn't broken her spirit, just knocked her off balance and made her a little insecure. The room blurred with a wave of nostalgia and misty eyes for "Addy," the name Mrs. Greenspaugh had insisted Rikki call her. She shook her head and searched for a tissue.

Rikki hadn't done nearly enough laughing in her lifetime, and with good memories and her favorite movie in tow, she'd decided to do some catching up tonight.

Just after the nurse had poked her and started the IV, the donation process began. She settled into her chair, and was about to start the movie.

A familiar voice made her freeze.

Dr Hendricks? She bent her head forward and looked around the donor equipment just enough to see his athletic frame. Pale blue dress shirt, navy slacks with leather belt on a trim waist…really terrific rump… Exactly what he'd been wearing that morning when he'd chewed her out.

What was he doing there? Surely he wasn't a donor. She sat back and tried to become invisible.

Unfortunately, even with several other loungers available, he chose the one right next to hers. Her heart did a quick tap dance, and she held her breath. Why did he make her so anxious?

He nodded at her.

She nodded back, resisting the urge to play with her hair.

Before she knew it, Dr. Hendricks had loosened his tie, unbuttoned his collar, and started rolling up his sleeves.

Rikki reminded herself to breathe.

He glanced at her, and his brow furrowed.

She squirmed, wondering what he was looking at.

"You don't usually wear your hair down at work."

"No. We're not allowed to." She ran jittery

fingers through near waist-length tendrils. Her thick, naturally wavy hair was the one physical feature she was most proud of, but under his scrutiny she doubted even that measured up to his high standards.

"I see," he said, giving no further sign of interest and snuggling back in his chair. "OK, Sheila, hit me with your best shot."

The blood donor nurse smiled. "With veins like yours, I could do it blindfolded."

"Don't get any ideas."

He'd obviously been through this routine before. The ease with which he spoke to people at Mercy Hospital impressed Rikki. She wished she had half of his confidence.

"Well, I gotta tell you, your hair looks a heck of a lot nicer like that than that floppy knot thing you wear at work."

She'd taken a shower and washed her hair after work, and realized that it was almost long enough to cut off and give to Care to Share Your Hair. The organization that made wigs for chemo children required ten inches. Soon she'd have to make an appointment to get it all cut off, but right now it took every bit of control not to preen over his backhanded compliment.

She shot him a mock offended look and caught a sparkle in his playful green eyes. Playful? Dr. Hendricks? Wasn't that an oxymoron? Time stopped for the briefest of moments, and it rattled her.

"Leave her alone," Sheila broke in, and offered a grin to Rikki. "He's just a big tease," she said as she tightened the tourniquet, flicked his vein with her finger and rubbed it with topical disinfectant.

"Well, you should see her, Sheila. Sometimes she sticks pencils in the bun, like chopsticks."

The nurse jabbed him with a large needle. He grimaced. "OK. I get your point. I'll shut up now."

"You should be ashamed of yourself. Rikki? Don't you dare let him do his imitation of Hank Caruthers."

Go, Sheila! Why couldn't she have such poise where Dr. Hendricks was concerned? But, hey, he'd noticed quite a bit about her at work. She fought off a smile.

Sheila finished her job and gathered her equipment to discard. She stopped briefly, growing serious. "How's your brother doing?"

"Things could be better. He's finishing up more chemo, so I wanted to make sure he had plenty of platelets available."

So handsome doctors who seemed to have it all together had brothers with cancer? Her heart tugged. She'd been focused on her own circumstances too much. No one made it through life without challenges, and Dr. Hendricks was no exception.

"I didn't realize your brother had cancer," Rikki said.

"Yeah, well, he's putting up a good fight."

"What kind?"

"Leukemia."

Her hand fisted on the soft rubber ball the nurse had given her to hold throughout the donation process. She forgot to let up, and her knuckles went white.

A few moments of strained silence followed. What else could she possibly say? *I'm sorry?* What did it matter how she felt about his brother having a life-threatening disease? She meant nothing to Dr. Hendricks.

"Has he considered a bone-marrow transplant?"

"He's adopted and no one in our immediate family is a match for him."

"I'm on the National Marrow Donor Registry. Have our lab check it out. I think there's a one in forty thousand chance he'll find a match."

Dane gave her a surprised but pleased glance. "That's a good suggestion. Well, we'll see how this next round of chemo goes."

Rikki gathered he didn't want to discuss the topic any further, and pushed the "play" button to start the DVD—anything to help distract her and chase away the awkward silence.

He stretched his shoulders and popped his neck before settling down.

"My daughters wear shoes just like that. Aren't they called Mary Janes?"

She glanced at her feet. "Yes." She flexed and pointed her toes. She'd spent one entire afternoon looking for her size of the unique shoes on the online auction network.

"I buy them for my girls because they're sturdy and have good support. Why do you wear them?"

"I like them?"

"Why don't those lacy black tights go all the way to your feet?"

How old was he? Didn't he know that leggings were back in? "They're leggings. They're not supposed to."

"I see."

If I don't look at him, maybe he'll leave me alone. She fidgeted with her hair.

"That's an interesting look with your denim skirt."

No luck. She tried not to sigh.

"I think my grandfather used to own an Argyle sweater like the one you're wearing."

Growing more uncomfortable each second with his examination of her style of dress, she tried to divert his attention. "It's the retro look. So, how old are your daughters?"

"Four."

"Both of them?"

"That would make them twins."

"Ah. Right. How nice."

"Nice? It's a nightmare. I mean, what am I supposed to do with two little girls? They want to play house and dress up and have tea parties. What about football? Playing catch?" He scrubbed his face. "Before they grew hair, I'd never tied a bow in my life. Now I'm forced to be a ribbon expert."

Rikki sputtered a laugh. "Can't your wife help?" She glanced at his empty ring finger, but that didn't necessarily mean anything these days. What if she'd said the wrong thing?

His casual expression changed along with the tone of his voice. No longer jovial, he spoke softly. "I'm a single father."

She'd gone and done it again, taken a friendly conversation and ruined it, just like her last foster-mother had told her. *You always ruin things, Rachel Johansen. Learn to keep your mouth shut. You're lucky to have a place to live.*

She restarted the movie and wished she could disappear.

"What are we watching?" Dr. Hendricks sounded like himself again. Was he giving her a second chance to put her Mary Jane clad foot into her mouth? Well, if he thought her style of dress was strange, he was bound to make fun of her quirky choice in movies.

"*Monty Python*," she mumbled.

He grinned. "Good choice. I see we're members of the same cult."

She looked at him with surprise. He winked, and a quick flutter burst across her chest. Positive the simple gesture hadn't meant anything to him, she wished she could resist his charm half as easily.

Nurse Sheila came by and checked both of their arms. "Are these IVs OK for you two?"

Rikki nodded and smiled.

Dr. Hendricks glanced at one of his arms. "'Tis but a flesh wound," he said with a poor excuse for a British accent.

Rikki's quiet laugh drew his attention. She saw that spark in his gaze again, and it jolted her. Thick dark lashes that any woman would die for lined the green of his eyes. If it weren't for the fact that he wore small wire-framed glasses, he'd be flawless. But wasn't that part of what she liked so much about him, the fact that he wasn't quite perfect?

The next time he made her feel nervous at work, she'd just imagine him sitting on the floor, legs crossed, playing dolls with two little pixies. Her mouth twitched at the corners.

Rikki relaxed. And if he enjoyed the humor of *Monty Python*, he just might understand her quirky personality. Something about that possibility made her break into a smile.

He caught her. They grinned at each other, and her heart broke into another tap dance. The quick rush made her mildly giddy, and she liked it. And there was that look again.

"I believe," he said, removing his glasses and looking steadily into her eyes, "I owe you an apology."

CHAPTER TWO

AFTER a day off on Friday when Rikki rested, rehydrated herself, and spent quality time with Brenden, she arrived at work on Saturday morning invigorated and ready for duty. It was a hell of a way to spend her birthday, but she didn't have any other plans. The call light in 408 was already on at the nurses' station—the fractured pelvis lady.

Rikki flopped her clipboard on the counter and headed for the room. Her hunch was right and she discovered the usual suspect on the call light. But the woman wore a worried expression, and pointed towards her roommate, the fractured femur in bed B.

She rushed to the restless and coughing patient.

"What's up, Mrs. Turner?"

The woman squirmed and pulled at her hospital gown. Her left leg, suspended by traction and a splint, had been healing beautifully, considering the hardware sticking out of it. She hadn't complained of pain the day before yesterday when Rikki had last taken care of her.

No one had mentioned any complications with her condition in report, yet here she was, clearly in distress. Rikki needed to figure out what to do.

"Are you all right?"

The woman nodded her head and fussed with the sheets on her bed, trying to adjust her position but unable to move much with the traction holding her in place.

As it was the beginning of the shift, Rikki took vital signs. Mrs. Turner had an elevated temp and her pulse rate was close to one hundred. She breathed as though she was anxious, short and shallow. There was no obvious sign of infection at the surgical site.

Something caught Rikki's attention when the woman tugged on the neck of her hospital gown. A sprinkling of small purplish spots dotted the surface of her chest. Rikki peeked inside the loose short sleeve of the gown, where more spots could be seen under her arm and on the side of her breast. It wasn't a rash. A mental red flag went up.

"May I look in your eyes, Mrs. Turner?"

The agitated woman nodded.

Rikki gently pulled down the lower lid and discovered a few more of the same sort of spots inside the eye membrane. Another red flag.

"I need to call your doctor, but in the meantime I'm giving you some oxygen." She pulled the two-pronged plastic tubing out of the bedside bag and connected it to the wall oxygen, then fitted it inside the patient's nose. "I'll be right back."

She rushed past the roommate, thanking her on her way out while dredging up well-learned data from nursing school.

Fat embolism was a complication that sometimes occurred with severe multiple fractures, especially of long bones. Mrs. Turner had a fractured femur. Fat globules could be released from the fracture into the bloodstream and act the same as blood clots, which could migrate to the lungs, heart, or brain. If not dealt with immediately, they could prove lethal.

Rikki grabbed the patient's chart, remembering Dr. Hendricks was her doctor. Flipping quickly through the hospital phone book, she found his private line and dialed. She'd try calling him before the on-call doctor.

"Dr. Hendricks," he answered gruffly on the first ring.

"Doctor?" She was surprised he was in his office on a Saturday instead of in surgery. "Mrs. Turner in 408B has developed petechiae across her chest and inside her eyes. She's restless and her temperature and respirations are elevated. I'm worried it might be fat embolism. Can you take a look at her or shall I call your on-call resident?"

"I'll be right there." He hung up before Rikki could explain why she hadn't thought to call the doctor on duty—because she'd become flustered and her mind had gone blank when she'd seen whose patient Mrs. Turner was. Rikki rushed back to the patient's room to check the oxygen saturation, which to her relief was in the normal range.

Dr. Hendricks appeared out of nowhere, winded and ready for business, as though he'd taken the stairs from his first-floor office rather than wait for the notoriously slow elevator. His sandy dark blond hair looked disheveled, and his white doctor's coat wasn't buttoned.

"Mrs. Turner." He slowed his pace and had a calm smile on his face, though his breathlessness gave his sprint away. "How are you feeling today?"

"OK, I guess."

As he casually questioned his patient, he looked under her lids and peered down the neck of her gown, confirming what Rikki had told him. "Are you having any chest pain or trouble breathing?"

Mrs. Turner shook her head. "I'm just antsy. You know, anxious, because I've been stuck in this bed too long."

"I'd go a little stir-crazy, too, if I were you." He nodded at Rikki while he listened to Mrs. Turner's lungs through his stethoscope. "Take a deep breath," he told the patient. "Does it hurt when you breathe?"

"No, I just feel like I need to cough."

"Let's get a blood gas, stat," he said to Rikki. "How is her urine output?"

"Um…" Rikki hadn't thought to check her intake and output, and Mrs. Turner hadn't asked to use a fracture pan yet that morning.

He didn't wait for her response. "Get some IV fluids going—normal saline, 125 cc an hour. Get a urine sample to check for fat globules. I'll order a stat CT scan of the brain and lungs, and we'll start heparin therapy after the blood gas has been done. Page me as soon as the results are back."

Rikki flew out of the room and paged the respiratory therapist for the blood gas test, then rushed to the supply closet for what she'd need to start the intravenous line. She glanced over her shoulder and saw Dr. Hendricks scribbling on a green doctor's order sheet, and blanched when he glanced up and caught her. When he smiled and nodded, she flushed and scuttled back to the patient's room, trying not to feel flustered under his smoldering gaze.

In the midst of setting up the IV bag and tubing, Dr. Hendricks appeared in the doorway again.

"Here's my beeper number." He handed her a small piece of paper.

She snatched it with an unsteady hand. He didn't let go of his end of the paper, forcing her to tug and look up at his teasing eyes. He gave her a casual smile and said, "Good catch. This could have gotten ugly. Oh, and I've ordered IV steroids."

"You'll be fine." He called out to Mrs. Turner. "Rikki here will keep tabs on you until I get back."

He nodded again, and smiled in a naturally sexy way that made her toes curl, then left.

She stood quietly, shaken. Why did she let him have such power over her? Damn, denial was useless—she had a crazy crush on the man. There was no getting around it.

Thankfully, she had something to distract her, something much more pressing to attend to than Dr. Hendricks's make-your-knees-knock smile. She had a sick patient to care for.

Dane had finished his weekend rounds and discharged several patients. Mrs. Turner's computerized tomography revealed early evidence of fat embolism in her lungs, and she needed to be transferred to ICU and intubated until her condition came under control. If Rikki hadn't been on the ball, the patient's prognosis could have been much worse.

He put his hands in his pockets, deep in thought, and walked to his car in the doctors' parking lot. He glanced up to find a captivating vision before him. Rikki's hips swayed with a mesmerizing rhythm as she walked quickly to her car. She'd unwound her bun and, as if a pendulum, her ponytail kept counter-time to her strut in a most alluring way. He rushed and caught up with her.

"What's your hurry? Hot date?"

She spun around, looking surprised. "Oh."

He could get used to that wide-eyed liquid brown gaze of hers.

She'd changed into baggy camouflage pants and a tight T-shirt, revealing a modest chest. Her backpack matched the pants. Not exactly the sexiest outfit he'd ever seen, but on her it worked. The fashion statement was further evidence that he couldn't deny: he was a good ten years her senior. Could they possibly have anything in common? At least she wasn't wearing combat boots, just brown high-top canvas sport shoes!

"Um," she said, as though still trying to figure out what to say. "No. I have some errands to run."

"I see." He forced her to slow down, so they could walk together and talk. "Where are you parked? I'll walk with you."

Painful silence made Dane more uncomfortable than he'd been in ages. Had he forgotten how to make conversation with a woman? He definitely needed to get out more. Well, he could always keep the subject on business. "Again, I want to thank you for being on the ball with Mrs. Turner."

"Oh, you're welcome, but it's my job."

"And you do it well."

It was never a good idea to socialize with people at work, especially with the kind of thoughts Rikki Johansen put into his mind. But his daughters had a sleepover party that night, and he was free to have some adult time. Only problem was, he didn't have anyone to spend it with. And seeing the ortho nurse had given him an idea. Ah, hell, why not just dive right in?

He cleared his throat. "If you're not busy tonight, how about having dinner with me?"

The color drained from Rikki's face. She practically stumbled before coming to an abrupt halt, though she covered it well by searching the asphalt for the invisible stray rock that must have tripped her. "You want to have dinner with me?"

"I believe that's what I said."

More stunned silence.

"Are you involved with anyone?" he asked.

"Well, no. But…" She bit her lower lip.

"I know, it might be considered improper of me to ask you out, but it's not like I'm your boss or anything. We may work for the same hospital, but I don't sign your checks, and it's just dinner, you know?"

"I'm parked over here." She pointed to an older and well-worn car. "Um…"

"Listen, if I've put you on the spot, forget I said anything, OK? No hard feelings."

"No. It's not that." She glanced briskly his

way, as though torn about what to say, and dug into her backpack for her car keys.

An odd feeling of discomfort prompted him to do more explaining. "I enjoyed watching the movie with you the other night, and I thought we'd started to get to know each other at the donor center. You seem like a nice woman and, bottom line, I don't feel like eating alone. That's all I'm saying."

He didn't want to pressure her into feeling obligated to go out with him. Though usually any woman he'd asked out jumped at the chance. Damn, had he gotten that rusty in the last few months?

Rikki still hadn't located her keys, and dug into several different pockets of the backpack in a frustrated manner. So how could he get out of this awkward mess he'd made and still save face?

"I'm not on call, but I gave you my beeper number earlier today. If you change your mind, beep me. I'll keep it turned on, just for you." Let her think whatever she wanted about the double meaning of "turned on." She *did* flip his switch—that, he couldn't deny.

But he had his pride. He'd dump the dinner invitation in her lap, and if she didn't follow through, he'd know she wasn't the least bit interested and forget about it. But, damn, he could have sworn there was something, some kind of chemistry between them. He'd definitely felt it. And he really did want to explore where it all might lead.

Maybe he'd been wrong?

He reached into his shirt pocket for his business card and handed it to her. "Don't lose that number." He attempted a dashing smile while feeling strangely insecure. "My cell phone number is on it, in case I don't answer my beeper."

She read the card and recited his number. "OK." She scratched her nose. "I'll see how things go."

Not the most encouraging answer in the world, but he'd settle for it.

No fancy automatic car opener for Rikki, she shoved the key into the lock, swung open a creaky and dented door, and slid inside behind the steering wheel. He noticed a child's booster seat in the back. Did she have a kid?

Right this minute he didn't care if she had three kids, he just wanted to take her out to dinner and have a good old-fashioned date with a woman. This woman. Male pride made him take the last word. "I know the perfect place for a great meal."

Before she could answer, he spun around, stuck his hands in his pockets and strolled slowly toward his new car in the doctors' parking section. He casually whistled, and hesitated long enough to make sure her clunker of a car started.

By six o'clock Rikki had grown restless. Nothing remotely interesting was scheduled on TV. She'd seen all of her DVDs a million times, and wasn't inclined to rent anything new. Her best friend had a rescheduled blind date she couldn't get out of, and had promised to celebrate her birthday with her on Sunday night.

Brenden sat quietly on the floor, playing with his favorite toy robot in his Superman Halloween cape.

She flounced down on her couch and put her fuzzy slippers up on the coffee table. Another

Saturday night at home—but this time, it was her birthday.

She couldn't get Dane out of her mind. Wasn't he totally out of her reach? Had he really said he'd liked talking to her? Well, they'd had a good time watching the Monty Python movie, and they'd both laughed at all the same parts. She imagined his chiseled face. What would his close-cropped hair feel like to run her fingers through? Ha! As if she'd ever have the chance.

His beeper number repeated in her head. How often did mature gorgeous surgeons invite her out to dinner? Never!

Meghan, the teenager next door, had offered to watch Brenden as a birthday present—why not let her?

Oh, what the hell. She searched for his business card, and a sudden rush of jitters made her drop it twice. She stood tall and swallowed, picked up the phone as a stream of adrenaline trickled through her chest, and dialed.

When he answered, she realized she'd been holding her breath. "Dr. Hendricks?"

"Call me Dane. What took you so long?"

How had he known it would be her? She picked at her hair, flustered. She heard children's voices and lots of racket in the background, wherever he was.

"Daddy? Daddy?"

"Hold on a second, Rikki. OK, girls, behave tonight. Emma, don't be a tattle-tale about everything Meg does, OK? And Meg, don't give Emma anything to tattle-tale about."

She heard him kiss his daughters, and another woman's voice spoke up. "Don't worry, I'll take good care of them," she said. "We're going to play dress-up and bake cookies and watch movies."

What sounded like a herd of little girls clapped and squealed, "Yay!"

Rikki smiled. She'd never been to a sleepover party. Come to think of it, she'd never played dress-up either.

More kisses. More goodbyes. A door closed.

"You there?" Dane asked.

She snapped out of her memories. "Yeah."

"When shall I pick you up?"

Ever cautious as a single woman, she answered without thinking. "I'll meet you."

After he'd told her the location of the restaurant, a place she'd never be able to afford on her own, her nerves doubled.

Now it was her turn to play dress-up.

Dane sat at the bar at his favorite steak house in Beverly Hills, nursing a beer. He'd pulled some strings to get a last-minute reservation. It was an unusually warm evening for early November, thanks to the Santa Ana winds blustering through L.A. He almost left his sport coat in the car, but remembered that the restaurant required men to wear jackets.

He tapped his foot and checked his watch again. He'd always been a stickler about being on time, and it was a quarter after the hour. But with that old clunker of hers, Rikki may have broken down on the way. He should have insisted on picking her up, but something in her tone of voice had made him back off and let her call the shots. He dug into his pocket for his cell phone and scrolled through previous incoming calls to find her number. Just about to dial, he glanced up.

Rikki stood in the restaurant entry in a whirl-wind of color. From her gauzy layered skirt to the two-toned baby blue and brown vest top, she lit up the room. Copper-colored sandals that laced around her calves reminded him of a film he'd once seen on the Roman Empire. He smiled.

She quickly brushed her hair to fight off the windblown look and glanced his way. He pushed off from his barstool and walked closer. He adjusted his glasses to take a closer look at the pleasing sight.

There were no less than six bead bracelets on both of her wrists, alternating blues with browns, and a necklace of several strands to match just about anything in the world. His daughters loved to make their own jewelry with plastic beads, just like hers. And right now he could almost see her in one of Meg's tiaras.

She blinked in recognition and her gaze skittered from his to around the lobby and back. In the upscale steakhouse, where women flaunted their highly insured gems, she stood out as "different." Well, to hell with everybody. He liked how she looked.

Rikki's quirky outfit tickled him. She was the most genuinely unique person he'd met in ages. A smile of admiration stretched across his face as he approached. Something about the intentional hint of brown lace from her bra peeking above her scooped neckline pleased him even more.

"Hi," she said, with an insecure gaze upwards. "I had trouble finding parking."

The expensive valet-only parking must have had her walking half a mile from wherever she'd left her car. Why hadn't he thought about that? He should have put his foot down when she'd insisted she'd meet him here. No wonder she was late.

"No problem." He reached for her hand and tugged her toward the hostess. "We're ready for our reservation." A surprisingly pleasant surge of energy started where he held her small, warm hand in his. He could get used to that.

She'd gone to trouble for him, and he liked the results. He glanced appreciatively into her delicately made-up eyes, more lovely than ever. Soft butterscotch waves tumbled over her shoulders, and she nervously used her free hand to flip her hair behind her shoulder. She smelled of citrus-infused lotion, and her tantalizing mouth glistened with lipstick, as if daring him to kiss her. Maybe he would…later.

Struck with a sudden urge to skip dinner and get right down to dessert, he swallowed hard.

"Your table is ready."

"You ready?" He broke off his stare.

Rikki nodded. He gave her a gentle nudge at the small of her back to move her along.

Her dainty hips swayed as they snaked through the crowded and noisy restaurant to their table. He liked the swishing sound the skirt made and the natural herbal scent of her hair.

Content with the thought of sharing dinner with his intriguing date, he couldn't help but think this could be the start of something. His mouth went dry and a quick response kept him from tripping on a chair.

When had been the last time he'd dared to think that?

Several patrons cast curious glances at Rikki. Maybe they thought she was some eccentric starlet, or a pop singer. Whatever their reasons for staring, she didn't let it faze her. Instead, she held her head high and squared her shoulders until the hostess seated them. He liked her attitude.

Rikki had never felt more self-conscious in her life. She'd only seen restaurants like this in movies. Perfectly coiffed women and tailored men filled the tables. She even thought she saw an actor from TV in one of the booths at the back.

No gawking.

Her multiple foster-parents had frequently brought in children for the extra income, not purely out of the goodness of their hearts, and a place like this would never be in their budget. She and a few friends had once splurged and treated themselves to a swanky restaurant when they'd graduated from nursing school, but she honestly didn't feel the food had been worth the price. She had her few favorite eateries, and they weren't anywhere near this side of town.

Dane looked relaxed and in his element while

he perused the menu. "I recommend everything except the seafood. Stick with steak tonight."

"But I'm a vegetarian."

He bore the look of a surgeon who had just amputated the wrong leg. He shook his head. "No wonder you're so scra—er, tiny. Why didn't you tell me?"

Bristling over his comment, she stared him down. "You never gave me a chance." She closed her menu and put it on the table. "You didn't give me a choice, or a say in where I'd like to go. You didn't ask what I'd like to eat. You just said, 'This is where we're going,' and 'Be there.'"

Dane stiffened. He clutched the wine list and frowned, confused.

She saw the evening turning around the wrong bend, and that was something she couldn't take. After all, it was her birthday. Didn't she deserve a nice evening out?

She wanted things to be better than this, even though Dane had some explaining to do about the look he'd given her when he'd first seen her. Surprise? Horror? She wasn't sure which. *Well, get used to it, buddy, because this is me. I know who I am, how I dress, and what I eat.* If he wanted to get to know the real her, she wasn't about to pretend to be someone else.

Truth was, she wanted a chance to get to know Dane Hendricks too—a man who would most likely never have given her a second look if they'd passed on the street. For some odd reason she'd caught his attention at work, and now she'd like to see how long she could hold it.

"But that's OK." She smiled brightly, changing tack. "They've got lots of great side dishes and salads." She picked up her menu again. "I'll be fine."

He studied her with a confused gaze a few seconds longer. "By any chance, do you drink wine? I was going to order a pinot…"

"Chardonnay?" She offered an apologetic smile. "I only like white wine. Sorry. But I can have tea, and you—"

"No." He raised his palm. "Chardonnay it is. And for the record, I like petite women."

Petite sounded a heck of a lot better than scrawny. Yeah, she knew what he'd meant the first time. But she'd give him a second chance.

Dane quickly made up for things. He became her hero when he withstood the snooty look the wine steward gave him when he ordered the bottle of white wine against the expert's advice for a nice pinot noir. No two-buck house wine for him, which was Rikki's usual choice when she was paying. He ordered the finest Chardonnay on the wine list. And he also suggested to the waiter that they should add a few more vegetarian entrées to their menu when they ordered their meal.

While they waited for their meal, Rikki skimmed her repertoire of conversational topics. The files were frighteningly thin when it came to holding her own with a man like Dane. What could they possibly talk about besides life at Mercy Hospital? An idea popped into her head. She adored kids. He had kids. Why not?

"So, you must love being a dad."

He raised his brows. "It's the toughest job I've ever had. Fact is, I'd rather do back-to-back hip replacements than stare into my daughters' big green eyes and tell them no."

He had a point. Children could be ruthless with their miniature bodies and precious faces, and the thought of big Dane Hendricks being defeated by his daughters made her grin.

"Don't get me wrong. I love my girls. And it's my responsibility to be their dad. But do I love being a father? I'll be honest with you. No."

"Well, I love kids. Someday I hope to have a whole houseful of them."

"You may change your tune once you've had a couple." He shoved a piece of bread into his mouth and chomped vigorously.

"I'm a foster-parent. I've hosted half a dozen kids already, and right now I'm caring for a four-year-old orphan named Brenden Pascual. It's been tough, but very rewarding to know that I'm giving him stability when his whole world has been turned upside down."

"That's commendable. You seem to be a very caring person."

"Nah. It's just my way of giving back."

"May I ask you a practical question? What about child care? How do you manage that? I've had nothing but trouble with nanny after flaky nanny. And my mother can only handle the girls for so long."

"Why haven't you tried Mercy's child care? It's open for all employees. That's the reason I transferred over from St. Michael's."

He tilted his head. "You know, you've got a point. Maybe I will try it out. Thanks."

She sat a littler straighter. "Glad to be of service. And for your information, caring for foster-kids hasn't put me off kids at all. I still want several kids of my own one day."

"That's also very commendable. But as for me, I know my limits. I've met my quota. No more kids."

Despite their differences on views of family size, the rest of the meal was pleasant enough. They chuckled over their favorite scenes in movies, and realized they both liked to hike. Rikki discovered Sheila was right—Dane did a flawless imitation of Mercy Hospital's administrator.

The absurdity of him clowning around and his spot-on imitation set her off giggling until she realized people were staring. She used her napkin to cover her mouth and quieted down. Dane kept taunting her by whispering more

Hank Caruthers-isms. He obviously enjoyed watching her squirm and snort.

After the meal they both agreed that pie was the only true dessert and decided to share. She didn't let on it was her birthday, and cake would be more appropriate. But she had to admit so far it had been a fairly decent date.

So why was she still feeling so uncomfortable with Dane?

After one large bite of mixed berry pie, a couple brushed past their table, and a familiar face from Mercy Hospital stopped.

Exquisite Dr. Hannah Young, sleek, statuesque, dressed to knock out whoever her date was in a tight little black designer dress, paused to rest her hand on Dane's shoulder. "Greetings. Fancy meeting you here," she said, as though it was some sort of inside comment about the restaurant being their favorite hangout.

Dane stood up quickly, dropping the napkin from his lap. "Hey, Hannah." They smiled warmly at each other and shook hands. She cast a cool dismissive gaze in Rikki's direction. "You know Rikki Johansen from Orthopedics," he said, and gestured toward her while he bent down to retrieve his napkin. Rikki had never seen him flustered before.

The doctor raised her eyebrows and tilted her head in Rikki's direction. Her message came through loud and clear. *What are you doing here with this gorgeous man? There must be only one reason. Hmm.* She made a quick calculated head-to-table glance, and her perfectly shaped brows twitched in disapproval. "Good to see you."

Rikki forced a smile, nodded and said a curt "You too."

"Well, I'd better get back to my date. See you Monday at the admin meeting, Dane. I hear Hank has another groundbreaking announcement."

"I'll be there." He passed Rikki a mischievous sideways glance as though on the verge of another imitation. "Hey, great seeing you, Hannah." Dane sat back down with new color in his cheeks. Was he embarrassed being caught in public with someone like her?

All the insecurities she'd tried to suppress for

the night came charging through her shaky defenses. As always, she didn't measure up. Everything had been a mistake. How could she—an abandoned kid from foster-care—ever feel on an equal footing with Dane?

"Why can't you be like those other girls, Rachel Johansen?" her least favorite foster-mom had chided her when she'd begun express-ing herself by dressing differently than her peers. "You ain't got no class and you never will."

She stopped in mid-bite of the last of the dessert as a wave of anxiety took hold, and pushed back her chair. "I need to find the ladies' room. Will you excuse me?"

He looked surprised, the way he'd looked when he'd first spotted her waiting in the restau-rant entryway.

She didn't give him a chance to say anything. When she reached the full-length mirror in the restroom, she scanned herself head to toe. No perfect little black dress for her. No. How had she possibly thought she looked nice with her own rendition of urban fairy? All she needed was a laurel crown. What had she been thinking?

She should have known better than to venture out of her safe little antisocial cave. But wasn't this how she'd always thumbed her nose at society? *Dress weird, be an individualist, show them you don't give a damn what they think. You don't want to fit in. Maybe they'll believe you. And while you're at it, maybe you'll convince yourself.*

But she did want to fit in with Dane.

Part of the dinner had been great fun, but at other times she'd sat stiff and self-conscious. Old habits never died. In each new foster-home she'd had to make a quick study of the family dynamics in order to survive. Her overall position anywhere she'd lived had boiled down to one thing—she had been a misfit. The families had either felt sorry for her, doted too much, making her withdraw, or had chided her for her mother's problems, expecting the worst. And when they had, she'd taken their challenge by messing up in school and dressing weird.

Rikki had quit intentionally failing in her studies once she'd been on her own, but the defiant style of dress had stuck even when she'd pulled it together and got the education she needed to become a nurse. It had become who she was—*different*.

If she was being honest, she'd admit that Dane had gone out of his way to try to make her comfortable. Hadn't he stuck up for her to the snooty wine steward and made her laugh with corny imitations?

Confused, she rubbed the line between her brows and paced. What should she do?

Her cell phone interrupted her thoughts. It was Meghan, her babysitter. "Brenden's throwing a fit," she said. "He keeps yelling, 'I want my mommy.' I can't calm him down."

Rikki took a deep breath. "He does that sometimes. I'm leaving right now. I'll be home within the hour." So much for trying to work anything out with Dane tonight. She'd go back to their table, explain the situation and hope for a reprieve.

When she got to the lobby, Dane had already paid their bill and was waiting for her. Obviously, he couldn't wait to get the date over with either. But his eyes were soft and he looked like a man seeking peace.

The truth about Rikki had been written on the bathroom wall. The mirror had said it all. She was a misfit and she and Dane didn't belong together. She needed to cut things off with him before they ever got started. And Brenden had given her the perfect excuse.

"Are you ready?" he asked.

She nodded.

"I thought we might go somewhere to listen to music or have a drink. What do you say?"

So he wasn't beating her out the door? It didn't matter—their date was history.

"I can't. My foster-kid is having a bad night." He wasn't the only one.

Dane straightened his shoulders and jiggled the car keys in his hand. "I see. Well, in that case, let me drive you to your car."

"Oh. No. That's OK. I can walk."

He reached for and held her elbow, not about to let her get away with her disappearing act. "Don't be ridiculous, Rikki."

Wasn't that what she was? Ridiculous? The whole evening had been a ridiculous farce, except it hadn't been funny. This was her life, out of sync with Dane Hendricks and the rest of the universe. And the damn thing was, she'd wanted to belong.

Rikki relented. "OK. I'm about a mile away, anyway."

He chuckled, and took her hand. "You're something else, you know that?"

Oh, yeah, she knew that.

Dane stared at Rikki, who studied her brightly painted toes while they waited for the valet to bring the car. No spark responded from her hand in his this time around. Instead, she'd subtly removed herself from his grasp in order to keep her hair out of her face when the wind had blustered through the driveway.

What the hell had gone wrong? He'd done all the right things for a perfect date—chosen a good restaurant, expensive wine. Hell, he'd even dressed up. But then, so had she…in a most unusual fashion. Peacock-feather earrings would have been the perfect accessories for her outfit. But he liked how she looked. Hell, he liked her, but somehow he'd only succeeded in making her uncomfortable. What had happened to the old Hendricks charm?

Despite every effort he'd made to loosen her up, she'd seemed uptight throughout dinner. He'd thought he'd broken through when he'd done his imitation of their hospital administrator, but she'd accidentally snorted when she'd laughed and had grown self-conscious again. He'd thought the snort had been kind of cute, but how did you explain that to a self-conscious woman?

And then, with exceptionally bad timing, gorgeous Hannah from Oncology had shown up, which had seemed to intimidate Rikki even more. But Hannah could do that to just about anyone. And to top everything off, of all the rotten luck, without knowing Rikki was vegetarian, he'd chosen a steak house. Way to go, Hendricks.

And what kind of convenient excuse was it for Rikki to claim her foster-kid was acting up so she had to leave? But if it was true, wouldn't he do the same thing if one of his girls were in need? Nothing was more important to him than their well-being. Fact was, children complicated life, and he didn't need any more problems. And Rikki couldn't hide that gooey-eyed look whenever the conversation turned to kids. Rikki was a package deal he wasn't sure he wanted to get involved with.

At a loss for words he tipped the valet and assisted Rikki into his car. She'd gone stiff again, obviously ill at ease. Did he need this kind of aggravation? Hell, no. He'd already had enough for a lifetime.

"So where're you parked?"

She cleared her throat. "Go down this street and make a right at the stoplight."

He tried not to chuckle at how far away she'd had to park in order to avoid paying a valet. She really did tickle him. Or maybe it wasn't the cost. Maybe she was embarrassed about her old clunker of a car and had worried it would stall for the valet. *Knucklehead. Why didn't I insist on picking her up?*

Everything was his fault. He'd let his physical attraction to Rikki dictate his actions without thinking things through. He should have gotten to know her better before asking her out. Truth was, they weren't suited for each other. At this stage in life he was looking for someone to relax with, so why get involved with a woman who was a revolving door for foster-kids?

Rikki Johansen was a reckless-dressing, do-gooder, overly sensitive younger woman, and he'd had enough women giving him trouble. He'd been left to raise his two girls single-handedly when their mother, his ex-wife, had discovered how difficult it was to be a parent. One unstable female per lifetime was enough and Rikki was obviously a woman trying to make up for something—and just like with having children, he'd met his quota. No. He didn't need any more problems. Next time he wanted a casual date, he'd ask Hannah.

Angry with the mess the date had become, he double-parked when they arrived at her car. He glanced over at her pixie silhouette, and against every ounce of etiquette he'd ever learned, a sudden urgent instinct took over.

The instant the car came to a stop, without further thought, he leaned across the bucket seat, took her face in his hands and planted a kiss on her lips. She went still under his kiss, but didn't pull away. The moment drew out while he felt her soft, plump mouth beneath his. She leaned toward him, kissing him back, her hand placed lightly on his cheek. He'd made the right decision.

Every ounce of logic flew out of his brain as he pressed closer against her warm, moist lips. Did she feel the spark? The intensity of the moment jolted him. He backed off.

Her ruffled gaze met his in the dark of the car, searching for an explanation. He couldn't say why he'd done it. She didn't ask.

"Rikki, I…"

Rikki cleared her throat and reached for the doorhandle. "Thanks for dinner," she said, breathless. The wind practically blew the door open for her. She jumped out so fast that she caught her necklaces and broke a strand, sending beads flying all over the street. She didn't stop to pick up any of them. It took both hands and all of her hundred-pounds-soaking-wet bodily strength to close the door.

Dane got out of the driver's side, only to have

Rikki raise her hand to wave goodnight. She slid inside her car faster than he could utter a sound of protest, and slammed the door.

After two false starts, while she refused to glance at him, her engine finally turned over, making a ragged metal and muffler song.

Speechless and confused, he slipped back inside his car, completely aware of the taste of her lips on his and her lingering herbal scent. He drove up the street, and watched through his rear-view mirror to make sure her car continued to run. She made an illegal U-turn in the middle of the road and drove off in the other direction.

He shook his head. *Women!*

The light changed to green. Something sparkly in the passenger bucket seat caught his attention. Damn, a reminder of the woman who'd managed to confuse him—a short strand of Rikki's fluorescent blue beads.

CHAPTER THREE

AT WORK mid-Sunday morning, Rikki's radar warned her that Dane was in the vicinity of the orthopedic ward. She'd lain awake half the night trying to figure out why she'd gotten so skittish with him. He'd been kind, attentive, even entertaining, but the restaurant had been completely outside her comfort zone.

Her lifetime of being carted from one foster-home to another had taught her to never get too comfortable anywhere. With the few families she'd cared about, she'd had to quickly learn how to let go. After a while it had gotten easy, especially if she never let herself get involved in the first place.

And Dane's kiss had struck like lightning, setting fire to her soul. Just the thought of it made her palms tingle. Out of self-defense she'd never allow herself to get comfortable with a man like him. She couldn't trust where it might lead.

Hearing his footsteps approaching, she dashed into one of her patients' rooms.

How could she ever face Dane again after last night? It wasn't anything he'd said. It was more what he hadn't said—the look he'd given when he'd first seen her in the restaurant lobby had told half of the story. The other half had come through when he hadn't bothered to tell her she looked great or even good, but she had sure read that approving gaze he'd given when Dr. Young had shown up. Just once in her life she'd like to be accepted for who she was inside, a person of value, not how she was wrapped.

"Nurse?"

She quickly realized she'd been hovering at the patient's door, watching and listening. "Oh! Hi, Mr. Tanaka."

Her patient had had a shoulder joint replacement and was being held captive in a torso cast with his left arm held at a shoulder-high salute and propped on a diagonal metal rod mounted from waist to elbow.

"How are you doing?"

She did a circulation check of his nailbeds, which checked out, and noted a pathetic look on his face.

"I need to take a walk. Will you help me?"

"Of course," she said. "Do you need to go to the bathroom?"

"No. I want to walk around the ward, to get out of this room. I'm going stir-crazy."

Oh, no. If she walked with Mr. Tanaka, she might risk running into Dane. But her patient had to come first, and if he wanted to walk, she'd assist him.

Rikki helped edge his legs to the side of the bed and swing them to the ground. She let his feet dangle for a few seconds while she covered his backside with another hospital gown. On the count of three she helped him to stand, and once he gained his balance and gave her the nod, they started on their trek around the ward.

Just as she'd feared, Dane still sat at the nurses' station, charting progress notes and writing orders. He glanced up before she could look away.

His brows lifted in a quizzical manner above his glasses, his stare steady with no hint of a smile. Was he thinking about the kiss, too? The sight of his handsome face and broad shoulders made her want to yell "Truce" and ask for "another chance" so she could explain why she'd lost all her courage last night. Surely, as a father, he must have understood she had a responsibility to Brenden first and foremost.

If she'd lost her chance at getting to know Dane because of that, so be it. She'd survived alone this long in her life, and she wasn't about to let a man like Dane throw her off course.

She blew Dane and his suspicious gaze off by focusing on Mr. Tanaka and his monster cast. Yeah, she'd take the easy way out.

"Why don't we make this walk a short one?" she said.

"No. If you don't mind, I want to circle the entire nurses' station," he said.

Feeling Dane's penetrating stare, she wished she'd worn her invisible uniform instead of the cornflower-blue scrubs.

She stayed by her patient's side to make sure

he didn't bump into anything or knock anyone out with a quick move of his arm and cast.

"Have I told you about my granddaughter, the doctor?" he asked while they ambulated.

She nodded. "Yes, but not recently." She pretended to be enthralled while the old man repeated all the same information he'd given her yesterday, wishing she had eyes in the back of her head so she could see what Dane was up to.

When they'd finally made it back to the door of the patient's hospital room, she felt a tap on her shoulder. She turned to find Dane unnaturally close and dangling a length of her homemade bead necklace. His eyes stared deeply into hers. She felt suddenly parched and steadied herself on Mr. Tanaka's cast. Why couldn't she just shrivel up and die?

"I thought you might want these back."

"Oh." Brilliant reply. She mentally kicked herself for getting so easily flustered where Dane was concerned. What should she do now? Her face went hot with embarrassment. *Keep busy. Act like that kiss never happened.*

As her hands were engaged, guiding her

patient, Dane tucked the beads into her smock pocket, never breaking his intense stare until he walked away.

With her heart sinking to her feet, she mumbled, "Thank you."

"Don't mention it," he said without looking back, dismissing her as thoroughly as she'd dodged him the night before.

Dane had presented her with intimacy she was far from ready to handle. Just the thought of getting involved with him made her toes curl.

She glanced at the beads in her pocket—so much for a fresh start. She'd never be able to mention her disastrous dinner with Dane to anyone. Unfortunately, the night of her twenty-sixth birthday would go down in history as a date to forget.

"So, as I was saying." Mr. Tanaka hadn't missed a beat. "My granddaughter, the doctor…"

On Monday evening, Rikki watched as long tendrils of hair got clipped from her head at the hairdresser's. Finally it had grown long enough to donate.

"Why are you cutting your hair, Rikki?" Brenden stood beside the pumped-up salon chair, watching intently as Randall did the honors.

"Because the Care to Share Your Hair program needs ten inches."

"And is it ten inches?" Brenden looked quizzically up at Randall, who nodded.

She'd read about the program last year online and had quit cutting her hair immediately. If she could make someone else's life a tiny bit better, she'd try. She glanced at Brenden's bright dark eyes, full of wonder. Wasn't that what it was all about? When you can't fix the state of your own life, help fix someone else's?

Brenden slapped his hands over his mouth and giggled. "You look funny."

"You think so?" Her hair could always grow back, but now that it had been cut, looking at a strikingly blunt and choppy style in the mirror, a whim popped into her head. Why not go all the way? "Can you cut my hair really short, Randall? I'd like to go spiky for a change."

"Sure thing," the hairdresser said. "Short is

always in," he said in an exaggerated manner to Brenden, razor-cutting several layers to frame her face.

Cringing at the memory of her disastrous date with Dane, she hoped he wouldn't recognize her the next time their paths crossed. And as most men liked long hair, she'd go one step further off his dating radar by wearing ultra-short hair.

It wasn't her imagination that there had been a spark in his eyes when she'd sat across from him at dinner. His handsome square jaw and straight white smile had made the back of her neck prickle on several occasions that night. A face like that belonged on the cover of *The Journal of Medicine's Hunk of the Year,* not behind a surgeon's mask.

And the kiss. She shook away the thought.

She had to give Dane credit. When she'd admitted how far away she'd parked the car, he hadn't judged her but had merely seemed amused. In fact, he'd seemed apologetic as if he'd wished he'd picked her up, instead of letting her talk him into meeting him at the restaurant.

Why couldn't she ever let people do nice things

for her? Because very few people had ever offered, and when they did, there were always strings attached. She wasn't a fool. He'd kissed her like he'd meant it. If she hadn't put a stop to it, he would probably have wanted to take advantage of her, sleep with her and never see her again.

But, wait, *he* had been the one to stop the kiss.

Oh, she could just die, remembering the sexy but confused look in Dane's eyes when she'd said goodnight and rushed out of his car as if she'd have turned into a pumpkin in another second. Things would never be the same between them, that was a given.

She glanced in the mirror and froze.

"Randall?" she said.

Deep in concentration, her hairdresser pursed his lips and primped and played with her rapidly shrinking hair. "Yes?"

"Are we almost done?"

"Yes." He lifted the long strands of what had been her hair. "This will make a beautiful wig." He laid them reverently on a special piece of paper on the counter and carefully wrapped them. "Let me get some hair paste so you can look sassy with your spikes. Do you like your itty-bitty bangs?"

"Let me see your itty-bitty bangs," Brenden chimed in.

It took all of her power not to gasp when Randall gave her a hand mirror to check out the back of her head. Definitely short. Outrageously spiky. Oh, heavens! But wasn't that what she'd asked for? She gulped and tried her best not to reveal her gut reaction. She made a second 360-degree sweep of her head with the mirror. OK, not so bad, just different. She'd get over the shock, she reasoned. "It's time for a change, Randall, and I *love* the cut."

"Now you look like me!" Brenden said, and giggled again.

By the time she'd gotten home that night, Brenden's bright disposition had changed. He'd become moody and restless.

"I want my mommy!"

Rikki peeled the boy off her leg and attempted to stand him on his own. He plopped into a heap, bumping his head on the carpet and crying more.

Rikki tried to get closer, but he rolled around and kicked at her feet. "I want my mommy!"

Knowing four was a stormy age for a child, and he'd most likely want to follow his will to the extreme, she let him be. What could she say—*you'll never see your mother again*?

After he'd made his desire to see his mommy and daddy unmistakably known, and had quieted down the tiniest bit, Rikki got a bright idea. Her only hope was what she remembered from her child development studies in nursing school—kids this age could suddenly change from sad to happy and back in a blink. A surge of optimism pushed her onward.

"Want to play a game?" She'd stocked her guest room, now Brenden's room, with children's toys for both genders, as she never knew what sex she'd get as a foster-parent. It was bright and colorful and, in Rikki's mind, looked like a happy place for any kid. Maybe if she could distract him, he'd calm down.

"No!"

Undaunted by his resistance, she dragged him, crying and kicking, as if dead weight, to the room and flipped on the light. He wiped away his tears. His favorite toy, a talking robot, blinked red eyeballs at him. "Want to play?" the toy said over and over at Rikki's command.

He giggled half-heartedly at Rikki's craftiness.

She handed him the remote control and he dutifully pushed a yellow button. The robot rolled toward him. Brenden pushed the knob again. It rolled closer. "Let's sing!" it said. "The farmer's in the dell…"

Normally, that part always made him smile, but not tonight. Unenthusiastically, he pressed the green button. The robot turned round in a circle, all the while singing the song. Brenden's eyes looked glazed and watery. His cheeks were flushed and his hair was damp.

Rikki felt his forehead with the back of her hand. He was burning up. "Let me take your temperature, kiddo. You feeling all right?"

"My tummy hurts." He rubbed his runny nose.

Sure enough, he had a temperature and was most likely coming down with flu. She got the children's antipyretic and gave him the proper dose, dressed him in his jammies, and helped him brush his teeth.

Rikki found a book to read about wild things and angry little boys who needed to settle down and go to sleep. She growled and roared and pawed at the air while she read, much to his droopy interest. Before she knew it, he'd cuddled into the crook of her arm in the rocking chair.

She read several more books, and had fleeting thoughts about how Dane must have felt as a single dad of not one but two daughters. He'd said it was the hardest job he'd ever had. She agreed, but it was well worth the challenge to make the world a better place. He wasn't shirking his responsibility to his daughters either. Just knowing she wasn't alone in the realm of single parenting, and then realizing that Brenden had drifted off to sleep, buoyed her confidence.

Barely able to lift Brenden's sturdy little body, she managed to carry him to his bed. She picked up the phone and dialed her nursing supervisor's sick call message machine. "Janetta? It's Rikki Johansen. I've got a sick boy here. I don't feel right about leaving him in the employee sick bay. I'll have to miss work tomorrow."

Once he'd settled into his pillow, she cuddled behind him to offer comfort. He was alone in the world, and deserved to know the security of his mother's arms. Rikki couldn't come close to filling that gap. Heck, she prided herself on being able to bring kids into a stable environment, take good care of them, and pass them on to better homes when the time came. She'd gotten quite good at it.

Brenden was an orphan with no relatives in this country. She herself may as well be an orphan—she hadn't seen her mother since she'd been three.

Rikki worried about getting too close to Brenden. The boy snuggled deeper into her embrace, and soon they both fell asleep.

Three days later, when Brenden no longer had a fever, Rikki bundled him up and brought him to the child-care preschool center at Mercy Hospital so she could go back to work.

"I'll come and have lunch with you today," she promised him.

The reticent boy shoved his thumb into his

mouth—something he hadn't done before—but didn't pull his other hand from hers while they walked toward the building. Perhaps he didn't feel completely back to normal?

"OK," he slurped.

As she approached, she recognized Dane's large, healthy figure, a tiny girl dangling from each hand. They looked up to him in adoration. One chatted non-stop. The other observed everything about her surroundings with wide pale eyes. Beneath similar dresses in different colors, they both had stringy legs with knobby knees. And, yes, both wore Mary Jane-style shoes.

Rikki tried not to laugh at the lopsided bows each wore on thin, straight blonde hair. Obviously Dane was still on a learning curve where hair grooming and accessories were concerned.

When he noticed her, he pulled in his chin and stopped. "Where have you been, and who have you got there?"

"This is Brenden. The little boy I'm fostering."

"Hi!" one of the girls piped up.

"Meg. We're not 'posed to talk to stwaingers," the other cut in.

"It's OK, Emma, I know Rikki," Dane said.

"I've been sick," Brenden piped up.

"So that's why you haven't been at work." Dane bent down to the boy's level. "Hi, Brenden. I'm Dane."

He'd noticed she hadn't been at work?

Brenden looked at Dane, not making a peep. His thumb slipped out of his mouth and he let go of Rikki's hand. "Hi," he whispered.

"He had the flu. But he's all better now, aren't you, Brenden?"

The boy dutifully nodded.

"I see. Well, Meg and Emma are new this week, maybe you can all be pals. OK, girls?"

Emma stayed put, shyly fidgeting with her dress. The more outgoing of the two, Meg, rushed to Brenden's side. "Come on. I'll show you my *favwit* toys. Do you like to play dolls?"

Brenden didn't seem to mind that a girl his age was taking his hand. "I have my own bestest toys."

He followed her inside. Once Emma decided it was OK, she took his other hand.

"I've got to get on the job," Rikki said, ready to make her break from Dane.

"Why did you cut your hair?"

Her hand flew to her neck. "It was long enough."

"Long enough for what?"

"To donate to Care to Share Your Hair."

"Oh, I've heard of that organization. Hmm. So let me get this straight, you donate platelets, register with the national marrow donor foundation, give your hair for wigs for cancer kids, and take in foster-children. Are you trying to replace Mother Theresa?"

She looked at her toes and gave a coy smile.

"Oh, and one more thing—you make your own jewelry," he added in a softer voice.

She sputtered a laugh. He hadn't forgotten their date any more than she had. "That I do."

"I'm still finding beads in my car."

They stared at each other for a few moments. Had he forgotten the kiss? Some sort of understanding passed between them. Respect? He'd made the best with what life had dealt him, and so had she. They had a lot more in common than she cared to admit.

Rikki scratched her nose, and wished she could think of something else to say. "I'll be late."

"Listen, if you ever need any sage advice on parenting, don't ask me, because I don't have a clue." He shrugged his shoulders and gave an all-forgiving smile.

"I'll be sure to put you at the bottom of my list." Maybe they could be friends?

"Thanks for recommending the child-care center. The girls have loved it so far."

"You're welcome," she said, feeling vindicated with a new spring to her step. "And if you should ever need more advice on child-rearing, I'll be glad to assist."

He smiled. "Have a good day, Rikki."

"You, too, Dane."

Just when she'd thought he'd left her life for good, he paused.

"By the way," he said. "If the warm weather holds, the girls and I are planning a day at the park on Saturday. Thought we'd take a short hike. Maybe you and Brenden would like to come along?"

"I didn't think we did so well with dating."

"Who said anything about a date? Think about it. If you change your mind, you've got my number."

Damn. Why did he always leave it up to her?

CHAPTER FOUR

FERNWOOD PARK had never looked so good that Saturday morning. Perhaps it was the pristine fall air. Or maybe it was the verdant hills with Chinese elm, sycamore, and those beautiful ancient oak trees. Rikki smiled, content. Then again, maybe it was the company of Dane and his daughters.

Above the park in the Los Feliz Hills sat the newly refurbished Griffith Park Observatory, as if a regal reigning queen. In awe, Rikki wondered why she didn't come to the park more often.

It had taken every ounce of courage to pick up the phone and call Dane, even though he'd invited her and Brenden to tag along with him and his girls. As before, he'd lobbed the ball into her court and waited for her return.

He'd sounded surprised Friday afternoon when she'd phoned, but pleased when she'd taken him up on his offer. She'd told him it was because she knew of an easy hike and a special cave she sometimes visited on her own, and she'd wanted to show it to Brenden. Dane had been gentleman enough not to call her on her prevarication, and had accepted her excuse for coming. This time she gave him her address and he picked them up.

It had been two days since she'd seen him at the day care center, and the power he still had over her nervous system surprised her. A swarm of butterflies had taken flight in her stomach when he'd tapped on her door. Seeing his handsome face again had almost made her need to sit down. Having experienced her skittish behavior at the restaurant, he'd seemed to know not to push. Today's get-together was nothing like a date. No pressure. It was just a simple outing with the kids.

She wasn't the only one who'd lightened up when Dane had appeared. Brenden showed more signs of life and excitement than she'd seen all week. Maybe it was the fresh air?

Once at the park, Rikki directed Dane to the best place to park and helped all three kids out of the car, handing each of them their hooded sweatshirts.

"We're going to go up this way." She pointed to a hiking trail. "You three hold hands. I'll show you my secret hiding place."

The kids danced around, excited, and ran ahead. "We're going to a secret hiding place!" Meg shouted.

"It's where I go when I need to think," Rikki said to Dane, remembering the many times she'd run off to her cave when she'd been a teenager.

Fifteen minutes later, after an easy hike, they reached their destination—a small meadow where a natural cave sat secluded in the side of a hill.

"This is my peaceful place," she said, gesturing to the surroundings.

Dane nodded. He wore jeans and a black T-shirt with a flannel, brown plaid button-up overshirt.

The children rushed Dane, asking for their toys—a ball and a Frisbee—and immediately ran to the meadow and started to play.

Rikki and Dane found a large rock at the

entrance to the cave and sat a careful distance apart, distracted by watching the kids play. The rich, damp earth smell had her taking a deep breath. Chilled air seeped out of the cave. How many times had the solitude here comforted her?

"This is beautiful. I can see why you like it here." It was the first moment they'd been alone since their date. "What do you think about when you come here?"

She shrugged and smiled, wondering if she dared to open up. "Trust me. You don't want to know."

"Try me."

She couldn't quite bring herself to tell him her deepest thoughts. Why unload her past on an unsuspecting man she hardly knew? It would only chase him further away.

"Why do I suspect it has a lot to do with all those things you do?" He pointed to Brenden. "And the reason you want to be a foster-parent? Most women your age wouldn't consider it. They're too busy dancing, party-hopping, and looking for the next good time."

"I guess it's because I'm a foster-care

graduate. I went to my first home when I was three. Just a little younger than Brenden."

"I see." He went on alert, a keen glimmer in his eyes.

He nodded and leaned closer. She could smell his spicy aftershave. Tempted to give in to his masculine appeal and tell him her whole story, she withdrew to the safe inner place she'd created early in life to help her cope. A place no one else could touch.

After a few moments of dead silence, he cleared his throat.

"About our date the other night…"

If Rikki hadn't known better, she'd think the usually self-assured Dane Hendricks had taken a nosedive into embarrassment. Had he thought about that kiss as much as she had?

She gulped and jumped in. "It was a little rocky. I'm sorry…"

"No. No. If anyone needs to apologize it's me." He took her hand in his. "I'm sorry I put you on the spot, that I picked a steak house without asking you, that I failed to put you at ease and, most importantly, that I kissed you when it was clear you weren't interested in me that way."

She wanted to protest—his kiss had made her fingers tingle—but found she couldn't quite form the words.

"I guess some people are just better off being friends," he continued.

Her heart sank with disappointment, but she knew he was right. They weren't suited to each other.

In the distance the girls' voices grew shrill, drawing their attention. They were fighting over a red Frisbee, neither letting go, one screaming, the other crying. Brenden looked on in silent curiosity.

Dane rushed them. "Knock it off, girls." His voice boomed through the fall air. The girls went quiet, staring at the ground mutinously.

Rikki skipped over and put a hand on each girl's shoulder. "Hey, you know what I do when I don't want to share?" The little ones looked up at her, still avoiding eye contact with their father. She could see the defeated look on his face. She needed to lighten the mood, and thought fast. "I play hopscotch! Come on, we'll all take turns."

She led them from the grass to a dirt and gravel patch and used the toe of her hiking boot to draw the hopscotch lines, then searched for a small rock to be her marker. "Go on, you guys find your markers."

With the tense scene totally forgotten by all but Dane, the children scuttled around, searching for their very own marker. While they did so, Dane touched Rikki's shoulder.

"Thank you for that. I just feel I have to shout over them when they start arguing. Damn, I'm bad at this parenting business."

"No, you're not. You just haven't found your parenting style yet. It might work better to get their attention if you lower your voice when you get upset. They'd have to quiet down to hear what you say, and they'd see by your facial expression that you aren't happy with them."

"How old are you? How do you know all this stuff?"

She laughed. "I paid attention in child development in my pediatric nursing studies. That's all."

Dane shook his head and gave a smile. It buoyed her outlook on just about everything. The kids tugged on her hands, and she ran off to play with them.

A few minutes later the children were ready for tossing the ball and she left them alone. Dane sat on a small boulder, grinning at her. Her step felt light, though she wore heavy duty hiking boots.

"Something tells me you're a special lady."

"Oh, no, not me. Besides being a notable date-saboteur, I'm just a regular girl."

He gave a soft smile and scooted to one side of the rock so she could join him. "Not so. For one thing, you're stoic. Most of the women I've ever known lay it all out there. You hear their history whether you want to or not. You know what I mean?"

She tried not to grin at the implication that all women were yakkers. "I'll forgive you the stereotype."

He chuckled and tugged on the short hair at the nape of her neck. Soothing warmth tickled her shoulders. The caring gesture made her long for something.

"So, do you want to tell me about what it's like to be a foster-kid?"

Could she trust Dane with her truth? With every sad detail of her childhood? It would only make him feel sorry for her. No, she'd keep her past to herself. "You don't want to ruin our day, do you?"

Dane got her point. Rikki had no intention of opening up. "For the record, I have issues, too."

She lifted her head, surprised by his confession. "Hey, if I were a reluctant parent, I'd have issues, too."

He nodded. "I'm punching in the dark as far as the girls go. I have no idea how to be a good father. You saw how I screwed up just now. How am I supposed to prepare them for life?"

"It's the hardest job in the world. But hang in there. For the most part, you seem to be doing great."

Something about spending a non-date afternoon had opened Dane up. He kept talking.

"It's not just being a single parent either. I feel like I don't have any control over my life anymore. As a doctor, I'm used to fixing people. Break a bone? I can fix it. Need a new knee? I can give you one. But my own kid brother has leukemia and I can't help. I'm a doctor, damn it, and I can't help him. It drives me nuts."

"But there are doctors who can help him with his leukemia."

"Yeah. But his latest round of chemo hasn't helped much. It suppresses the disease, but his bone marrow doesn't respond well enough. They say he needs a marrow transplant and, like I said, I can't even help him there."

"You should have the lab tap into the hospital donor center files for other possible donors. And don't forget the national registry. Check mine out. It's worth a shot. There's got to be someone somewhere who matches."

He sighed. "Yeah. Good point. I'll look into it." After a few more moments he said, "Have you ever thought about tracing your birth family?"

His warm breath tickled the side of her face. She felt chills down her neck.

"Maybe you have relatives somewhere."

"It's a scary thought at this point. I don't know anything about them, only my surname, and it's pretty common."

"Maybe I can help you with it."

"Thanks." She pulled back and looked up into his green eyes. "Maybe I can help you find a marrow donor for your brother. I'll ask all the nurses on Four North to get tested."

He smiled down at her. "You've got yourself a deal."

After a long delightful day, the warm weather cooled, and the kids had played themselves to exhaustion. They made a fast-food stop for dinner and said their goodbyes on her doorstep while Dane's daughters slept in the car. Brenden ran inside to use the toilet.

"I'm having a few neighborhood kids over tomorrow afternoon for a craft day. Maybe your girls would like to come? We'll be making simple decorations for Thanksgiving. They might enjoy it."

"You know? I'd really like to watch some football with Don tomorrow. I may take you up on that offer."

The next afternoon, Dane dropped off his daughters as planned. He looked rugged in old jeans and a worn shirt with his favorite football team's name on it. While he was distracted, saying goodbye to his girls, she took in every inch of him. Damn.

Later, when he tapped on her door, Rikki felt excited. Her heart fluttered and her cheeks warmed up. All the other children had gone home with their Pilgrim and turkey decorations made from toilet-paper rolls, glue, and colored construction paper. Meg and Emma were watching Brenden show off all the cool moves his robot could make in his bedroom.

"Hey," Dane said, on the other side of the screen door.

"Hiya." She opened it and let him in.

"So you survived?"

"I had six kids from the neighborhood, plus your girls, and I've got to tell you, Meg and Emma are really good kids. You should be proud of yourself."

"They didn't fight?"

"They were perfect angels."

"Are we talking about the same kids? Short, blonde hair, knobby knees?"

She laughed.

Dane's softened eyes crinkled when he smiled down at Rikki. She caught her breath, realizing he intended to kiss her. He dipped his head and gave her a gentle, warm kiss, covering her mouth for what seemed like eternity, but in reality lasted only a moment or two. Her head spun with the feel of his lips on hers.

Just as quickly, he backed off. His eyes were a darker shade of green and his smile was nowhere to be found. He looked deeply into her eyes. "Oops. There I go again." He held up his hands. "I know. We're just friends."

Reeling with the kiss, and the possibilities, Rikki searched for her voice and strung together the best thing she could think of. "Just friends."

After floating through Sunday, reality came crashing down for Rikki on Monday morning. Brenden woke up sulking and stalled every step of the way getting ready for and going to child care.

Rikki had barely made it out of the shift change nurse report when Janetta summoned her to her office. Rikki peeked around the door and found her supervisor on the phone. Janetta waved for Rikki to take a seat.

Rikki stretched her neck and shoulders, sat, crossed her legs and waited for Janetta to hang up.

"You look about as perky as a dead cat. What's up?"

"I had a rough morning with Brenden. He didn't sleep well last night. Ever since he woke up this morning, all he seems to want is his daddy." She bit at a rough fingernail.

"Aw, all boys are alike. Just rough-house with him. He's a boy—he wants to be thrown around, not talk. I've got two grandsons, I should know."

"Hmm. I'll think about that. So you wanted to see me?"

"Yeah. I just received a call from the donor center. They're requesting an interview with you some time today. I'll try to find someone to cover for you so you can go down to the lab, but I can't promise."

"Thanks. But I'm sure whatever it is can wait. It's probably about my next platelet donation appointment or something."

Before she'd finished her thought, the ward

clerk's voice came over the intercom. "We need muscle in room 411."

Raising her brows, Janetta stood. "We'd better check this out."

They arrived in the room to find a patient in a long leg cast and a neck brace on the floor. An apologetic and wild-eyed nurse explained, "I was helping him onto his bedside commode, and we both lost our balance. You're OK, aren't you, Fred?"

"I'm fine. I just can't get up."

A male LVN entered the room, and the four nurses lifted the patient up and assisted him back into the bed.

"Be sure to fill out the incident report," Janetta said to the nurse as she left. "And call his doctor. He may want to get an X-ray."

The rest of the day was busy with nonstop admissions, discharges, and patient care. Rikki never had a chance to go to the donor center, and promised to see to it the first thing next morning. She was exhausted by 4:00 p.m. and wanted to go straight home. Brenden was cranky and withdrawn when she picked him up from day care. There would be no chance to relax tonight.

Rikki loaded up the boy into her car, secured him in the car seat, and drove home.

Two hours later, things hadn't gotten any better. Brenden whined and moaned, and every time Rikki tried to get close, he pushed her away.

Her home training suggested giving the child time to adjust to his new surroundings, but Brenden's break-in period seemed to go on for ever, and felt like torture. After a few weeks of smooth sailing, he'd had a relapse. And tonight he continued with his favorite demand.

"I want my daddy!"

She'd failed at trying to distract him with puzzles, books, toss toys, children's DVDs, and ice cream. Nothing worked to bribe him out of his mournful mood.

"I want my daddy!"

She raked her fingers through her hair and thought fast. Since she'd been doting on him, he'd quit screaming for his mother. She'd noticed how quiet and awed he'd gotten whenever Dane had given him attention at the park on Saturday. He especially enjoyed himself when they'd played catch.

Maybe if a man were around to give him some attention, he'd quit begging for his father. It seemed like wacky logic, but Rikki was desperate, and her young charge seemed beyond miserable. She had to do something.

"I want my daddy!" Brenden dissolved into a heap on the floor.

Rikki grimaced and picked up the phone to call the only man she knew—Dane. The kiss that had made her knees go weak came to mind and she had to sit down. He'd been in surgery, sending new post-op patients to her ward all day, so she hadn't seen him.

There was no answer at his house and, suspiciously relieved, she didn't leave a message.

She hoped she could distract Brenden by baking, even though it was the opposite of what Janetta had suggested. Horseplay?

"Let's make your favorite cookies."

"I want my daddy!"

She opened a cupboard and handed him a measuring cup. "Here, I need your help."

An hour later, managing to minimally engage the boy, the first batch of chocolate-chip cookies came out of the oven. She removed them to cool while Brenden watched with a blank stare. Someone tapped on her apartment door. She flung a dish-towel over her shoulder and rushed to answer.

Dane stood under the yellow porch light with both daughters in tow. The girls were dressed in pajamas, robes and slippers. One wore a Cinderella pattern, the other Sleeping Beauty. They looked tiny and vulnerable next to their huge father.

The sight of him made Rikki go off balance. Even Brenden lifted his head from his curled-up position, curious as to who was at the door. "Hi!" Rikki couldn't help her excitement.

"Hi," Dane said, with a serious face. "I need to talk to you."

"Something smells really good," Meg said.

"They're chocolate-chip cookies," Rikki said.

The girls rushed inside. "My favewit!" one of them said.

They ran over to Brenden, who quickly forgot about sulking.

"What's up?" Rikki asked.

Dane stepped cautiously inside her apartment. "I've just received a call from the hospital. They've found a donor for my brother."

"That's wonderful!"

He brushed his knuckles across her cheek. "You've got flour on your face." He stood quietly watching her, as though searching for the right words while she wiped at the smudge. "They found a donor with a matching cell type to Don's, and want to move ahead with the bone-marrow transplant as soon as possible. I got the call when I was giving the girls their bath a half-hour ago."

Her hand flew up to her mouth. "That's so fantastic."

"Once his current chemo treatment is finished, he'll be ready for the transplant. All we need is to get the consent of the matching donor."

"How soon will that be?"

Dane reached for her hand, his trembling slightly. "As soon as you sign the Intent to Donate."

Rikki stared at him, confused. Her fingers tightened in his clutch.

"I don't know why they called me instead of you first, but the head of the lab said you're the match. I think he tried to call you at work today, and he'll call again tomorrow. Or maybe he left a message here. I don't know, but I couldn't wait to tell you."

All the blood rushed out of her head. She'd been so distracted by Brenden's foul mood she hadn't checked her phone messages. Dizzy, she needed to sit down. He grabbed her arm and helped her to the nearest chair.

"I know this is a shock, but you're a godsend, Rikki. You're the one who told me it's a one in 40,000 chance and yet you match my brother. You're the perfect match. Isn't that incredible?" He grabbed her hands again and smiled at her.

Her mouth went dry. She tried to focus on Dane's face, but it was blurry. The process of donation had seemed so easy when she'd signed up with the national registry. While she was under anesthesia, a doctor would do a simple surgical procedure using hollow needles to withdraw marrow from her pelvic bones. Her marrow would be infused into Dane's brother and would travel to his chemo-suppressed marrow and would hopefully multiply and help him back to restored health. Wasn't that what she'd dreamed of doing when she'd signed up? Hell, she'd already committed to donating. What was one more signature?

Dane sat beside her and put his arm around her. "Think about it. Take as much time as you need before you sign anything tomorrow. OK? It's a huge commitment. If you agree, you'll need to get a medical exam. That's easily arranged. Listen, I'll watch the kids while you think this through."

On cue, the oven timer went off. Another batch of cookies was ready to come out. Without thinking, she jumped up and rushed to the kitchen to finish her baking. She'd attended a thorough information session when she'd originally signed up with the national registry, but it all seemed so distant. Now it was real.

Dane followed her to the kitchen.

Brenden took one look at him and blurted, "I want my daddy!"

Using potholders to remove the baking pan,

she said, "I can't seem to make Brenden happy tonight."

"Is there something I can do?"

"Maybe just talk to him? I honestly don't know how to reach him." She glanced over her shoulder. "But your daughters sure know how to make him feel at home."

"My social butterflies." He smiled proudly. "I know they didn't get that from me. What the heck, let me give it a shot. I owe you after yesterday."

Dane seated himself on her mini-couch, making it look even tinier. With her mind spinning about her chance to help someone with cancer, she brought out the first batch of cookies and a pitcher of milk. Slowly Brenden edged closer to the group, and wound up standing next to Dane, staring and quiet. Dane offered him a cookie. He took it and nibbled.

"Hey, champ. What's up?" Dane reached out his hand for a high five, but instead the boy crawled onto his lap. Dane bounced him on his knee until Brenden giggled.

"Stop it." Brenden chortled.

Dane stopped instantly, for one second, then started right back up again with the energetic bouncing.

"I said stop it." Brenden laughed.

"Stop what?"

"You know."

"Oh. OK." Dane repeated the teasing pattern several more times, to Brenden's delight.

The light-hearted gesture made Rikki smile, though she worried and was preoccupied about her important opportunity. It was time to put all her good intentions to the test. She suspected what her decision about donating marrow would be, but the details had to be worked out.

Brenden hadn't ever looked this happy. When Rikki realized Emma and Meg would soon be invading the game, she moved right in. "Do you know what I've got?"

"What?" they both asked.

"Beads! Would you like to make your very own bracelets?"

"Yeah!"

Rikki guided the twins into Brenden's room and closed the door, giving the males a chance to bond. An hour later, they'd all made new jewelry and then wore them for a special tea party, and she'd read three books to the girls while they'd cuddled up on the bed.

Rikki snuggled with them, content. They smelled like bubble bath. A strange feeling wrapped around her until she thought she might cry. These precious little girls, so eager for female attention, had brought her a new kind of happiness. It reinforced her dream of having a big family. The more the merrier. No child left behind, all loved equally. And their uncle needed a bone-marrow transplant so he could be around to watch them grow up, get married, and have kids of their own one day. Basically, it was a no-brainer. She'd already made her decision.

"I have to pee!" Meg said.

When Rikki opened her door, she found Dane with Brenden on his back, riding him around the living room, intentionally shaking him off, making the boy laugh hysterically, and then faking an apology. "Oh, I'm sorry, champ. I don't know how that happened. Here, get on again."

The moment the boy did, Dane bucked him off again. Brenden howled with joy. "Now, you stop that."

Rikki smiled so hard at the sight of them rough-housing and having fun, her eyes watered. Dane's brother deserved a chance at life. She'd sign the consent first thing tomorrow morning.

When the girls finished in the bathroom, they rushed their dad and Brenden.

"My turn."

"My turn."

They dove onto their father's broad, strong back, and all three of them rode around her house on a bucking bronco tour until Dane collapsed from exhaustion.

"That's enough, kids," he said breathlessly. He plopped onto his back and lay sprawled on her floor. He'd taken off his glasses. His shirt had become untucked from his pants, revealing a flat stomach with a thin trail of light hair working its way up to his chest. She shouldn't have noticed it, but she couldn't help herself. Not only was he one appealing male, he was a natural at fathering, at least the playing-around part if not the tying of bows.

"Would you kids like to watch a short video?" Rikki suggested in order to give Dane a break and keep him around a while longer.

"Yeah," they sang out, knowing it was well past their usual bedtime.

No sooner had she set up the kids with the latest children's show, and started to sort things out in her kitchen, than Dane showed up, leaning on her kitchen door. It made her nervous.

She tossed the dishtowel over her shoulder and folded her arms. "How can I thank you?"

"I was about to ask you the same thing."

"What?"

"Something tells me you'll sign that consent." He gave her a long, appreciative smile. "And I haven't seen my girls shine like that in a long time. You've got a way with my kids."

Wait. Was he flattering her to get her signature? He seemed so sincere about everything, and she'd already made up her mind.

He waited expectantly for her response.

"So do you. Brenden really came out of his shell tonight. I'll have to call on you more often."

Dane stepped closer, his hair disheveled from playing with the kids. Rikki resisted a powerful urge to fix it. They made silly grins at each other. He still wasn't wearing his glasses.

A subtle change of expression overshadowed his charm.

"Taking on more parenting duties is the last thing I need on my plate right now. So don't get any ideas. OK?"

Stung by the reminder, Rikki pretended not to care. "Ah, no. Brenden is my responsibility."

"As long as we've got that straight." He seemed defensive.

"I will need to go into the hospital for the bone-marrow procedure, though. I'll need someone to watch Brenden that day at least."

"You've already made up your mind? Of course I'll watch him. It's the least I can do." He took another cookie from the batch cooling and chomped it down. "You make great cookies, by the way." He stepped closer and took the towel off her shoulder, tossing it onto the counter.

She wanted to be angry with him for steam-rolling through with the marrow donation plans, and for being so blunt about never wanting more kids, but his close proximity made her heart race.

He put his hands on her shoulders. "For the record, I really liked how you were dressed the other night at the restaurant. I don't think I told you." His eyes bored into hers.

How could she stay mad at him?

"And I like your short hair." He took inventory of her spiky new look and smiled. "I like those hip-hugger jeans and this skimpy top, too." He tugged on the hem. "And right now, *friend,* I'd like to kiss you again."

Oh, what the hell. His green eyes sent shivers down her spine. Everywhere he touched, her skin prickled. She hadn't forgotten their kisses, either of them.

He pulled her closer and covered her mouth with a soft touch of his lips, just like the kiss the other night on her doorstep. She wanted to protest—it wasn't the right time for this—but it felt so good. She crumbled against his chest.

She went up on tiptoe, tilted her chin and kissed him back, sending a definite message.

He dipped his head, held her face with both hands and took possession of the kiss, investigating the tiny piercing above her lip with his thumb. He drew her closer. She wrapped her hands around his neck. He tasted like bittersweet chocolate as she ran her tongue along the soft lining of his lips. He slowly explored her mouth and melted away every last bit of hope that she'd be able to control herself.

A warm rush traveled over her entire body when, on a deep inhalation, their stomachs touched and she felt tingling down to her core. The pleasant awakening danced between her legs, up her spine and across her chest. Her kisses grew eager, and his hot hands roamed across her back and over her hips.

Her breasts tightened and peaked and she pressed into his firm chest to satisfy her need to be closer. He groaned, and caressed her tighter, while kissing the most sensitive spot on her neck. Shivers slid over every inch of her skin. Hot with desire and longing to feel more of his flesh, she reached under his shirt and ran her hands up his taut skin, lightly brushed in crinkly hair.

She had a strong urge to rip open his shirt and run her cheek across that hair, but controlled herself. Cheers from the living room made her realize the kids' video was already over. The last thing she wanted to do was end their embrace, but she kissed him once more then broke away.

"Want to have a sleepover?" *I only meant to think that!* She couldn't believe the bold words even as they came out of her mouth.

He tugged her back, hugged her close and kissed the top of her head. "Definitely. But not tonight. I've got surgery all day tomorrow, and its way past their bedtime. I'm going to have to take my girls home."

She totally understood and tried not to cringe. Determined to be more businesslike, she said, "You made such a difference tonight with Brenden. Thank you."

"And you'll make a huge difference for my brother."

She kissed his cheek, and regretfully pulled

free from the warmth of his arms, ready to get back on duty as a foster-mother. An uncomfortable thought came to mind. "You're not just doing this because I'm donating bone marrow to your brother, are you?"

"Hell, no! And I'm insulted you think so. I came over here to tell you the good news. All the rest is just as much a surprise for me as it is for you. Trust me. OK?"

Had she ever been able to trust anyone in her life? Mrs. Greenspaugh came to mind. *"You're a good person, Rikki, my girl, and you've got to understand, there are other people in the world just like you—good at heart. But we all make mistakes."*

Dane scratched the back of his neck. "I have to admit, I enjoyed myself horsing around with Brenden, too." His smile grew mischievous. "But not nearly as much as just now." He lifted his brows. "Horsing around with you."

She grinned and felt her face grow hot. She mock fanned herself. "If you keep that up, I'm going to need to put on the air-conditioning."

"A quicker way to cool down is to take off

your clothes." His eyes hooded over, and he scanned her from head to toe with what felt like X-ray bedroom vision. Oh, yeah, he liked what he saw.

"Rikki, I need you," Brenden called out.

In an instant, a completely different feeling blossomed in Rikki's chest—pure and simple joy. Something even more compelling than kissing a sexy man like Dane got all of her attention—her foster-son's voice.

CHAPTER FIVE

RIKKI straightened her clothes and burst through the door.

"Yes, Brenden?"

"Can you take the video out?"

"Sure."

"I like your friends." His smile, accented by deep dimples and chocolate-chip smudges, was the single most beautiful sight she'd ever seen. Dane's taut stomach ran a close second.

"Well, since you like us so much," Dane said, entering from the kitchen, "I've got Thursday afternoon off. Maybe we can all go and see a movie since Rikki will need to see a doctor."

After their kiss, her head went spinning with the possibilities. Things would get too complicated if they continued with their infatuation for each other.

"Are you sick, Rikki?" Brenden's face looked worried.

"No. I'm going to help someone else get better."

Dane said goodbye to Brenden, bundled up his girls, and sent a meaningful sexy look her way just before he put his glasses back on and opened the door. She fought off the magnetic force of his smile, and stopped herself from rushing over and planting another solid kiss on him. Instead, she hugged the twins and promised another tea party soon.

When she stood up, their eyes met.

"I'll never be able to repay you for what you're doing for Don."

She gave a somber nod. "I'm not doing it to get repaid. I'm just glad I can help."

"I know, but nevertheless…"

Brenden leaned against her leg. As natural as breathing, she ran her fingers through his shock of hair.

She allowed herself to wallow in her little happily-ever-after fantasy for a few extra moments before Dane's words in the kitchen came back to ruin her mood.

Taking on more parenting duties is the last thing I need on my plate right now. Despite what he'd said, he was only staying involved in her life because she'd said she'd help his brother.

"So, I guess I'll see you soon," he said, turning to leave. He glanced over his shoulder with a mischievous glance. "For the record, you really look hot tonight."

She grinned as they walked away, and then sputtered a laugh when she heard Meg ask, "Does Rikki have a fever?"

She closed the door and switched off the porch lights.

The possibility of she and Dane getting involved sent a shiver down her spine. First, she needed to learn how to feel comfortable around him, and to trust he'd accept her for who she was. She knew she wasn't in the sophisticated league of Hannah Young, if that was what he was looking for, but she'd never want to be like her. She didn't want to just be a fling to Dane either and worried that he was using her to make sure his brother had a bone-marrow donor.

Addy? Why can't I trust anyone?

A lifelong lesson in self-defense urged her to form a plan. As she was donating her marrow to Dane's brother, she couldn't get involved any further with him.

Her decision was for the greater good, and this good deed required both physical and emotional sacrifice.

Brenden tugged on her leg. "Will you read me a book?"

She bent down to meet him eye to eye. "Of course I will." She ruffled his hair, pretending nothing had changed when her entire outlook toward Dane would never be the same. "But first you've got to brush your teeth."

Dane sat across from Janetta the next morning. "I realize Rikki had a few days off last week, and she probably doesn't have any paid vacation due, so I'd like to make sure she gets a check."

"I don't have a clue how we can do that. The only thing I can do is to arrange her schedule so she has a three-day weekend. Maybe you can arrange for the donor date to match?"

"That would work. Now that she has consented

to the marrow donation, I've moved ahead and made all of the arrangements. It's an outpatient procedure." He rubbed his jaw. "She'll need a driver to take her home. I'll see what I can do."

Things had certainly gotten complicated. Rikki had gone from being the date from hell to his brother's savior, and he wasn't sure where his feelings fit in. She was so damn energetic and quirky, she kept him on his toes, and he liked being challenged by a woman. Not to mention her exemplary altruism. But she was already suspicious that the only reason he pursued her was for an ulterior motive—his brother's health.

Now that they'd kissed, his instincts about her being one damn appealing woman were right on target. He'd suspected as much on their disastrous date and again on that day in the park, but after last night he knew he wanted more of Rikki in his life. He'd have to work out all the other details later.

"Hey! Where did you go? You were saying?" Janetta said.

Dane snapped back into the conversation. "Oh, I'm just working things out in my head. I'll take a couple of days off work and reschedule a few elective surgeries to make sure I have time for both Rikki and Don. If she needs transportation home and someone to watch Brenden, I guess I'll have to do that, too. Hell, I owe her, and it's the least I can do."

"I'll say."

But it wasn't just his duty—he cared about Rikki, and wanted to make sure she was OK. Damn, that part had snuck up and knocked him sideways.

"By the way, this Thursday, she'll need part of the afternoon off. I've arranged for Dr. Prescott to give her a physical. If all goes well, we're good to go for the marrow donation on Friday."

"This Friday? Has she agreed to all of this?" Janetta sputtered her sip of forbidden coffee at her computer. "How am I supposed to do all the rescheduling now?"

"For the record, she is definitely on board with it. I'm sure you'll work something out, Janetta. You're the queen of scheduling." He stood to leave. He was due in surgery in fifteen minutes.

She rolled her eyes and shook her head. "Right."

"And maybe you and I can take turns calling her every couple of hours on Friday night. You know, just to make sure she's all right."

"Why don't you just have her stay with you?"

"Now, Janetta, that wouldn't be appropriate. The rumor mill would go into overdrive if anyone found out."

"Honey, I've got news for you, it already has."

On Friday morning Dane picked up Rikki and Brenden at eight o'clock. Her scheduled appointment for hospital admission was nine. He'd have time to deliver the kids to the child-care center and get back up to the surgical oncology suite before anything officially started.

Rikki appeared at the door freshly showered, and she hadn't bothered to put any makeup on or do anything with her hair. She looked all of sixteen with big brown eyes and pale olive-toned skin. Skin smooth enough to stroke.

He cleared his throat. "You ready?"

She nodded. "As ready as I'll ever be."

"You haven't eaten or had anything to drink since midnight, right?"

"Oh, gee, Doc, I didn't know that." She crossed her eyes, stressing her point.

"All right, OK, I guess I'm as nervous as you must be."

She nodded, put on her warm-up jacket and zipped it up. "Everything will work out."

An hour later she was in a hospital gown and was handed a consent form for the operation.

"You know, I've always had to explain these things to my patients," she said to the nurse. "From this side of the gurney it does look scary. I know they've got to state every single thing that might go wrong but, gosh, possible nerve damage and-or death?" She looked at Dane for support.

"Everything will go as smooth as silk," he said, resorting to clichés to ease his nerves. The palms of his hands had gone clammy at the thought of Rikki going through the procedure and, worse, any potential complications. "By the way, I'm calling in my staff privileges. I've asked to sit in on the marrow donation. Is that all right with you?"

She nodded, swimming in the hospital gown, looking as though she was shrinking right before his eyes. "I'd like that."

"I thought you could use some moral support." He gowned up. "I promised my brother we'd all celebrate with a beer once the transplant is a success."

"How long will that take?"

"Two to four weeks. We'll keep our fingers crossed until then. Come to think of it, some prayers wouldn't hurt."

The anesthesiologist arrived in the room with her box of drugs—a short, exotically attractive woman with large dark eyes similar to Rikki's, accentuated by the OR cap. "I'm Dr. Armerian." They shook hands. After a wide, infectious smile, she got down to the business at hand. "Are you allergic to any medications?"

"Not that I know of."

"Good. I'll be using general anesthesia as you'll be in the prone position. It works best."

She continued with a whole series of questions, and Dane felt like an eavesdropper, learning so much about Rikki's medical history. Though many of the family medical questions couldn't be answered as she hadn't a clue whether heart disease or high blood pressure and several other ailments ran in her family or not. Being a foster-kid, she just didn't know.

The oncologist, Jere Rhineholdt, stepped into the suite and greeted both of them. He was a middle-aged man with broad features, graying hair and slouching shoulders. If seen on the street, no one would ever dream the unassuming man was a highly acclaimed specialist. "Are you ready?"

Rikki nodded. The nurse started the IV, stuck on the electrodes for monitoring Rikki's heart, and placed the automatic blood-pressure cuff set for every five minutes.

Dane knew Jere had performed hundreds of these bone-marrow aspiration procedures and was as skilled as any doctor could be. Still, his heart raced when he realized there was no going back.

"Rikki, I'm going to sedate you now." The anesthetist injected a small amount of medicine into her IV port.

Without thinking, Dane placed his hand over Rikki's shoulder to reassure her. She glanced up with trusting velvet eyes, and his chest squeezed. She felt so tiny, and he had a powerful urge to protect her.

The RN edged in front of Dane. "Are you sure you being here is OK with Hank Caruthers?" she asked teasingly.

Dane grinned at the reference to Mercy Hospital's administrator—the king of policies and procedures. Sensing the tension in Rikki's body, and wanting to lighten things up for her, he couldn't resist doing his infamous, though politically incorrect imitation. He'd gladly resort to clowning around if it would help her relax.

Rikki sputtered a laugh, along with everyone else—mission accomplished. With her eyes closed, she yawned. She hadn't gone completely out yet. Within a few more seconds she was deep asleep and had been skillfully intubated by the anesthetist. Dane helped the nurse roll her onto her stomach, though, with her lithe body, he could have done it by himself with one arm tied behind his back.

The surgical nurse washed and prepared her skin with antiseptic and placed a sterile field across her buttocks. Rikki had a delicate butterfly tattoo on her right hip, and Dane's mind went flying off topic for a moment when he first caught sight of it. He quickly reverted to professional-ism, though his libido had definitely been piqued.

Dr. Rhineholdt donned double sterile gloves and reached for a scalpel. He made a tiny slit in Rikki's flesh above the right posterior iliac crest, her hipbone, and dabbed at a drop of blood with sterile gauze. He reached for a large-bore needle and used surprising force to ram it into her bone to collect spongy red marrow, reusing the small incision over and over as the point of entry.

Dane winced at each puncture. Thank God Rikki was unconscious. This step would be repeated two to three hundred times over the next couple of hours in order to collect a liter of bone marrow.

More blood beaded and trickled down Rikki's hip. The nurse repositioned a sterile towel to catch it. Rikki's tiny body got bumped and pushed with each collection, and Dane didn't think he could take watching it much longer. But he needed to be there for her. She didn't have anyone else, and he owed her. He took her hand in his, knowing she was unconscious and wouldn't even know. Somehow it gave him reassurance.

How different it was to be the surgeon and do what was necessary for the patient, as opposed to watching someone he cared about go through a tough procedure. He looked away as the needle was plunged into her hip again. What kind of person would go through this for a complete stranger?

Someone like Rikki.

After completing the procedure on the right side, Dr. Rhineholdt moved to her left hip and made a new incision. The marrow was collected into heparin-rinsed syringes and transferred to a container washed with anticoagulant to prevent clotting. An hour and a half into the procedure, they'd almost filled the bottle to the 900-milliliter mark.

Dane noticed Rikki's blood pressure and pulse slowly dropping. The anesthetist had noticed it, too. "Are we almost done?" she asked. "I may have to wake her up soon."

"I need a full liter for the best results," Dr. Rhineholdt said.

"Blood pressure 80 over 50, pulse 45." Dr. Armerian increased the rate of the IV.

A knot the size of a fist formed in Dane's stomach. *Wake her up. Come on.* Her respirations were even and the oxygen saturation was 98 percent. With the other vital signs so low, the oxygen reading offered little solace. He rubbed her palm with his thumb then stroked her wrist in an attempt to stimulate an increase in her heart rate.

The oncologist made another puncture and collected 5 ml more marrow. The alarm went off on the heart monitor. Forty beats a minute. Blood pressure 75 over 45.

Dane clenched his fist and straightened his back. He shot an intense look at Jere. The anesthesiologist didn't wait a second longer. She drew up and injected into the IV an antidote for each ingredient in the sedative cocktail she'd given Rikki earlier.

Dr. Rhineholdt made one final lunge, and when he was done the nurse placed pressure on the two tiny incisions over each hip crest using sterile gauze. When the bleeding had stopped, she applied a bandage to both sides. The incisions were so small there was no need to stitch them.

Each ring of the monitor alarm robbed the air

from Dane's lungs. He was responsible if anything went wrong with Rikki. He couldn't bear to have that on his conscience. So what if they didn't have enough bone marrow to complete the donation? Hell, it could be the difference between a successful bone-marrow transplant for his brother and a failure. Damn.

Slowly the monitor numbers edged upward, and Dane could breathe without a hitch in his chest. Rikki squeaked a moan around the endotracheal tube. The sweetest sound he'd ever heard from the toughest trooper he'd ever met— all five feet and one hundred and one pounds of her, according to her chart.

He stayed by her side throughout recovery, and was there when she asked for a sip of water.

"Hi," he said as he handed her the straw.

She sipped and swallowed. "Hi," she said with a hoarse voice and droopy eyes. "How did we do?"

"You did great. They're treating your marrow even as we speak, and Don should be getting the infusion tonight."

"That's great."

"You're great." He cupped her cheek with his palm. She gave a dry-lipped smile and sipped more water. Only because the recovery room nurse showed interest in the attention he gave Rikki did he stop. His attachment to the orthopedic nurse was none of her business.

The same recovery nurse monitored Rikki's vitals and when she noticed Rikki was fully awake said, "Doctor wants you to stay in the hospital overnight for observation."

"But I don't want to stay. I want to go home."

"They want to make sure your blood pressure doesn't go too low. You're only 90 over 60 right now."

"That's normal for me. I've got Brenden to look after. Please tell him to let me go home," she pleaded.

Reading the frustration on her face, Dane said, "I'll talk to him…" and left her bedside.

Fifteen minutes later, after pulling more doctor privilege strings, he reappeared, smiling victoriously. Rikki had fallen back to sleep, but her eyes popped open with an expectant, woozy stare when he touched her hand. "Well?"

"Dr. Rhineholdt said you can go home in a couple of hours on one condition."

"What's that?"

"That you come home with me."

"I can't do that!"

"Weren't you the one who wanted a sleep-over?" he whispered with a sly smile.

Rikki wasn't about to let anyone know how dizzy she felt when she stood up. She used the recovery room bed to support her.

Once the nurse had gone over the discharge sheet and warned her about possible side effects from the procedure—the main one being fatigue, followed by back pain, with dizziness running a close third, oh, and don't forget to watch out for signs of infection—she signed the sheet and stood to dress.

The back of her hips ached as though she'd hiked twenty miles straight up and hadn't drunk enough water.

The orderly arrived with a wheelchair, and she gingerly slipped into it. Every bump and jiggle got her attention. She finally accepted the fact that there was no way she could watch Brenden by herself tonight.

Dane waited at the hospital curb with all three kids safely tucked into their booster seats in the back of his weekend car, an SUV. Her eyes widened at the sight of a typical family man, arms crossed and waiting, at the front of the discharge circle. He wore casual slacks and a yellow form-fitting polo shirt—an unassuming work of art.

A quick fantasy about her big family dreams eased the pain in her lower back. But she couldn't let herself go there. Maybe someday with someone else, but from now on she'd keep things with Dane on a strictly professional basis.

Dane rushed to her aid and helped her to stand, then guided her with a strong, secure hand to the car. He treated her as if she was fragile and precious, and the thought gave her chills.

"Hi, Rikki!" all three kids blurted in unison once she was seated in the front passenger seat.

"Hi, kids!" She gave a special smile to Brenden, who looked as if he was thriving with his new friends.

"We saw the penguin movie yesterday, and

Dane said we could rent a movie tonight," Brenden said with an excited grin.

"Yay!" Meg screamed, quickly mimicked by Emma.

The twinkle in Brenden's eyes made Rikki's throat tighten.

Dane got into the car, filling up the entire driver's side. "Are we ready?" He smiled as though they'd known each other all their lives.

"Yeah!" the kids' choir squealed.

Oh, yeah, her fantasy world responded. *I'm definitely ready for this.* If only this could have happened under different circumstances.

She dozed on and off during the drive until a short twenty minutes later they arrived at Dane's high-rise condo complex on Los Feliz Boulevard. She'd often driven by the two towers at the base of the Los Feliz Hills, but the only thing she'd ever thought about it was how the buildings stood out against all the other apartments and condos along the boulevard. She'd always assumed that Dane would live in a house.

They parked underground, and with Dane's assistance Rikki was able to get out of the high cab and wait while he released all three of the kids from their seats. "Hold hands," he said, obviously repeating a several-times-a-day mantra without a second thought.

"Come on, Brenden, we'll show you our toys!" Meg whisked the boy into the elevator and Emma announced she'd pushed the tenth floor button.

A comforting hand around her waist and another under her elbow made her feel as if she'd just come home from giving birth or something. Now, that was a fantasy she'd save and savor some time as a dream prayer just before she fell asleep.

"Watch your step," he said, when they reached a single step. "Hold the elevator open, please, Emma."

She liked how he spoke to his daughters with respect, not dictating their every move.

The girls were well versed in condo elevator skills, and the door remained open until Rikki and Dane were safely inside. Then Emma pressed the "close" button, and they were on their way.

At a loss for words, she leaned comfortably into Dane's strength and warmth, a healing touch no pain medicine could ever provide, until they reached his floor. Just for now. Tomorrow she'd straighten him out on their new business-only status.

They entered a bright living room lined in subtle wallpaper with several oversized modern artworks decorating the walls like exclamation marks. Real oil paintings without frames—no prints for him.

The kids dashed down the hall.

Dane guided Rikki to a sage green wraparound leather couch that felt like kid gloves when she sat on it. One entire wall was filled with glass, and the light filtering through felt warm on her face. No drapes were in sight.

A small balcony with two lounger chairs faced the length of Vermont Avenue. Off in the furthest distance, thanks to the recent sweep-through of Santa Ana winds, a hint of sparkle made Rikki realize she was closer to the Pacific Ocean than she'd thought.

"Wait here while I get your bed ready."

"I don't need to lie down," she protested.

He stopped in mid-step and gave her an authoritative stare. "Yes, you do."

While she waited, she glanced into a small open kitchen area with kid-functional dining table. Next to it stood a sturdy, multicolored plastic children's toy kitchenette extravaganza. Rikki's heart squeezed at the thought that Dane's daughters came before any false pretense of adult sophistication.

Back in the living room she noticed he'd staked out a personal corner with an overstuffed recliner chair and reading light. A super-large TV filled up another part of the room. Functional, unclut-tered living at its finest, and Rikki approved.

Dane reappeared with a pulse-jolting smile. "Your bed's ready."

"My bed?"

"Well, it's my bed, but you can use it today. I had my housekeeper put on fresh sheets just for you."

Her mouth went dry. He went out of his way with clean linen for her?

He assisted her to stand and led her down the hall. On the way they passed an office, the girls' room, where the kids were happily engaged in play, and a guest room. Wait, didn't she belong there?

He opened double doors into a cavernous master bedroom with a king-sized bed. No less than a dozen pillows lined the head, and the covers were turned down. Simple pale blue sheets waited.

She stopped short. "You didn't have to go to all this trouble on my account. I can sleep in your guest room."

He shook his head, looking exasperated with her self-effacement. "Just get in and shut up, will you?"

In her sweet dream about being a princess, Rikki crawled through what felt like molasses to get to an ornate door. She touched it and entered a foggy world of white, scented by tomato soup. Her stomach growled with pleasure. Someone tapped on her shoulder.

She squinted open her eyes and peeked. It was dusk, and Dane stood at the edge of his bed, a tray in one hand.

"I thought you should eat."

She sat up, vaguely remembering the dull pain in her hips, and ran her fingers through her hair. What must she look like? Did it matter?

"That smells dreamy. I'm famished."

"Good." He set up the tray over her lap, and sat beside her. "Brenden is having chicken strips, potatoes and peas with the girls. That boy can eat."

Rikki grinned. "Tell me about it." She forced a steady hand in order to take a spoonful of soup. She slurped and swallowed. "Tastes great."

"I didn't know if you wanted something more substantial or not, but I could throw a cheese sandwich together if you—"

"This is perfect. I can't thank you enough."

His eyes softened into a smile. He looked as though he was about to say something, but refrained.

"Dad?" Meg appeared at the door. "Brenden wants thirds."

"I'll be right there." She rushed back down the hall, repeating the news, while Dane tilted his head and lifted a brow. "Were you starving that kid?"

Rikki sputtered a laugh. "I think he has a hollow leg."

His eyes lingered on her. "I like when you do that."

"Do what?"

"You make a cute little snort when you laugh."

"I do not."

He stood. "You do…and it's cute."

Before she could protest further, he'd left and shut the door.

An hour later, she'd managed to clean up and walk down the hall. Dane sat in the midst of three rambunctious kids, playing a board game. The skilled orthopedic surgeon looked bewildered by the rules. His glasses where shoved to the top of his head. He rubbed his jaw.

"No, Dad. You're s'posed to take your turn *after* you spin the thingy, *then* you look at the card. Not first," Emma said, with arms crossed and an impatient stare.

Brenden covered his mouth and giggled.

"Hey," Dane chided. "Us guys have to stick together."

Brenden laughed harder and ducked his head.

Rikki's heart lurched at the sight. For someone who refused to have any more kids, he was a natural father. What a waste. But it didn't matter, because they were only business acquaintances from here on out.

Brenden noticed her first. "Hi, Rikki. Are you all better now?" The girls rushed her and threw their arms around her waist. She almost lost her balance.

"Careful, girls," Dane said.

Though stiff and achy, she smiled and hugged them. "Yep. I'm fine."

Dane jumped up. "Can I get you some water or tea?"

"I can get it myself. You go ahead and finish your game."

He tossed her a thanks-a-lot glare. She stuck out her tongue, smiled and walked to the kitchen to fill the teapot.

A short while later she felt him enter before she saw him. The fine hair at the base of her neck prickled. He leaned against the refrigerator in his socks. No wonder he'd snuck up on her. "I don't want you to push yourself too much tonight."

"Honestly, Dane, I'm just a little sore. No big deal." She scanned the cupboards to avoid looking into his eyes. She couldn't allow her infatuation with him to grow a centimeter deeper, and those bottomless green eyes might force her to. "Where are your teabags?" She reached for the logical cupboard closest to the stove at the exact instant he reached for the knob. His hand covered hers and held tight. Chills marched a two-step up her arm. She'd never been so physically drawn to a man in her life. Damn it! Why did it have to be under these circumstances? "This one?"

He stared at her and moved closer. "Right here." He opened it, still not releasing her hand from his, and reached over her with the other to retrieve the tea. "I have to tell you, you look great in my bathrobe." He rubbed his jaw. "I'd like to see you in one of my pajama tops, but I don't own any." His mouth slanted into a taunting smile.

Shaken to her core, she used the counter to regain her balance. Did he sleep in the buff? Why was he tormenting her? With her face on fire, she reached for a glass for water.

He knew what he was doing. He was taking advantage of her vulnerable state, and the thought of sharing his bed made her toes curl.

"I feel a little dizzy. I think I better sit—"

Before she could finish her sentence, he whisked her off her feet and carried her to the couch. His strong arms wrapped her in security and, with his heat and strength, thrilled her to her very center. His masculine scent sent her reeling. No! She couldn't let this happen.

"Don't move," he scolded. "I'll bring the tea to you."

She spent the rest of the evening trying desperately to keep her distance from Dane. Once she'd accidentally drifted off to snooze and had used his shoulder as her personal pillow. He hadn't pulled away.

Later, they all watched children's movies until her eyes grew heavy and she gave in to sleep. The instant her eyes closed, Dane picked her up and carried her, like a crippled princess, back to bed. It felt fantastic and she didn't even think about protesting. Only for tonight, she promised herself.

Made snug and comfy by Dane's expertise with the blankets and pillows puffed just so, within minutes she drifted off into a deep sleep.

Some time in the early morning hours she woke up with her back pressed against the natural warmth of Dane's broad chest.

CHAPTER SIX

HAD he crawled into bed with her? His hand rested on her waist and one leg was protectively across her thigh. Fearful of what she might find, Rikki lifted her head and looked over her shoulder. Dane was on top of the covers and fully clothed but, still, how had he wound up there? She hadn't told him he could share the bed. Would he assume such an intimate notion? She savored the feel of him, just for a second, and almost dozed off again.

Under most circumstances she'd never agree to sleep with someone she hardly knew. But hadn't she thrown herself at him a few days back? Considering the extraordinary circumstances that had cast them together, they'd become close very fast, both professionally and personally. But she'd made up her mind about keeping their relationship strictly professional. She really should do something about Dane sleeping beside her.

Soon.

An hour later, after she'd dozed off another time or two, she cleared her throat. He gave a deep, contented inhalation. She cleared her throat again. He stirred and stretched long muscular arms. One eye popped open. He went up on his elbow, looking as surprised as she felt. His gaze darted over her, around the room, and back to her face, as though trying to get his bearings.

"Um. You're probably wondering how I got here," he said, reading her mind. She'd never seen Dane look sheepish before.

She rolled away from his grasp, leaving enough room for his twins plus Brenden to crawl between them. Pulling the covers tight to her chin, she faced him. "As a matter of fact, I was."

"You don't remember me bringing your pain medicine last night?"

"No." Was he fudging?

Recovering his composure, he yawned and

rolled onto his back, folded his hands behind his head and stared at the ceiling. "You groaned like you were in a lot of pain, so I stuck around until you settled down. Only problem was I got comfortable on my favorite part of the bed." He pointed to the opposite side of the king-sized bed. "Way over there." He was now lying in the middle. "I guess I dozed off and must have migrated toward your warmth during the night."

Her warmth?

He glanced at her with an apologetic twinkle in his sleepy eyes.

"I'd say I was sorry, but I'd be lying." He gave a charming grin that would have knocked her socks off if she'd had any on. "This was so much better than sleeping on the couch."

She pulled the covers tighter to her chin. Why had all her bravado disappeared? Hadn't she been the one who'd requested a "sleepover" the other night at her apartment? But this was different—he'd actually slept in the same bed as her. And she'd just recently made up her mind about keeping whatever it was they had going on all business.

The implication slowly sunk in of the two of them lying together on his bed, and Rikki almost jumped off the mattress. She would have if she hadn't been tucked in so tightly and her hips hadn't still been tender.

He sat up. "Look, I'll give you some privacy. You can shower while I fix breakfast. You can even lock the door if that makes you feel better." Within a flash he'd left the room, leaving Rikki to wonder if it had all been a drug-induced dream. Nah, she couldn't have conjured up the penetrating warmth and sublime feeling of his broad chest spooned against her back, even if she'd tried.

The memory sent shivers all over her body. She couldn't dance so she made "snow angels" on his sheets, choosing to linger under the covers just long enough for the chills to settle down.

She'd get a hold of herself and, as hard as it would be, she'd make sure Dane understood from here on out they were nothing more than two people trying to get his brother well.

Dane had enough time to make a pot of coffee before the kids woke up. What the hell had he been thinking? He never should have sat on his bed and waited for Rikki's pain medicine to kick in. He'd woken up in a totally compromised position, and Rikki probably thought he was taking advantage of her. Never in a million years did he want to do that. He respected her too much.

Had he really thrown his leg over her thigh?

Like clockwork, the kids got up, and ringleader Emma switched on Saturday morning cartoons, taking his mind off thoughts of Rikki. Emma plopped onto her stomach, her head propped up on her elbows. Brenden, who'd slept in the guest room where Emma had thrown open the door on the way down the hall, followed. And Meg sandwiched herself in between them on the living-room floor.

The dynamic trio. What a sight. A thought flickered in the back of his brain. Was it a good thing or a bad one for his girls to become attached to a foster-child? They'd experienced enough loss in their short lives. How would he explain it to them if Brenden's relatives appeared and took him away?

He'd offer the kids cereal and save the last

two eggs for Rikki's omelet. Orange juice and toast would be enough for him.

Damn, she'd felt great beside him. It had been ages since he'd cuddled up with a woman, and he hadn't realized how much he'd missed it until last night...with Rikki. He poured himself a cup of coffee and took a swig. Maybe it was time to think about having a woman in his life again. That was, if she was interested, he could get used to sharing a bed with her.

But what if things didn't work out? How devastating would it be for his daughters to lose another mother figure? Was it worth the risk of getting involved with Rikki?

When she sauntered down the hall, showered and completely dressed in her warm-up suit zipped up to her neck, the girls rushed her. "Hi, Rikki! Are you all better?" They hadn't wanted a hug from him that morning. Were they so starved for female attention?

She smiled and gathered both of their heads to her waist. "I feel great today." She played with their fine and frizzy hair and got down on her knees to look them both in the eyes. "Hey, may I comb your hair and braid it?"

"Yeah!" They jumped up and down. The poor girls had forgotten what it was like to have a woman fix their hair.

Brenden looked disgruntled.

"Hi, Brenden," Rikki said. "May I comb your hair, too?"

"Nah," he said, pretending to be annoyed yet looking pleased she'd asked. "Just do theirs. That's girl stuff." He put his chin back on his palms and watched TV.

Rikki found the girls' brush and started with Meg's hair, slowly brushing and smoothing her thin shoulder-length waves. Emma stared in reverence, patiently waiting her turn.

Dane pretended to be busy making toast, but he watched from the corner of his eye. Meg sat rapt under Rikki's spell, letting her part, divide, and gently tug her hair into compliance. The result: two spindly blonde braids and a bright smiling face.

His heart tugged at the sight.

"I want my hair like that, too," Emma said.

Rikki repeated the ritual with Emma. Dane wondered what was so hard about taking care of little girls that his ex-wife couldn't handle? What had proved overwhelming to her seemed second nature to Rikki. The simplest gesture of braiding hair, made both of his daughters ecstatic. And she'd managed to make sure Brenden didn't feel left out either. Three kids, all satisfied.

Though so young, Rikki was a natural mother and shouldn't be robbed of the chance. And he was a man who'd met his kid quota. Not exactly a perfect match. He needed to think things through before he made a huge mistake.

She glanced his way with velvet brown eyes and caught him staring at her. All his doubts flew out of his head. The fact was, her mothering turned him on. How sick was that?

She blushed—another thing she did regularly around him—which also turned him on. She'd put the sexy piercing back in, and his mind drifted to that special little butterfly tattoo on her hip.

Holy hell, what was he thinking at eight in the morning?

He raked his fingers through his bed hair and turned away. Thank God the toast was done.

Later that day, Dane's mother offered to watch the kids so he could take Rikki to meet Don.

His brother was in isolation on the second floor oncology unit at Mercy Hospital, so they washed their hands, gowned up and put on masks and gloves, before entering his room. The chemo had suppressed his immune system, and the biggest threat to the success of the bone-marrow donation was infection.

Rikki tried to keep her shocked reaction to Don's frail appearance from reaching her eyes. Though closer to Rikki's age than Dane's, he looked several years older and was completely bald from chemotherapy. Her heart lurched at his fragile condition. She prayed her bone marrow would help him turn the illness around.

When they entered, Don brightened up. His wide grin, straight teeth, and a cleft chin could have tricked Rikki into thinking they were blood brothers. But Don had been adopted.

"Hey, bro," Dane said, natural as a daily

routine. He lightly punched his brother's arm with a soft fist.

"Is this my match?" Don's eyes looked expectantly toward Rikki.

"Yes. This is Rikki Johansen," Dane said proudly.

She reached for Don's extended hand. "It's so wonderful to meet you."

"Hey, you're the lady of the century in my mind."

"Oh." She blushed, and Dane wrapped his arm around her shoulder. She glanced up to admiring eyes, but saw something deeper and it made the hair on her neck prickle. She couldn't let things between them go any further.

Since donating marrow, being left in Dane's care, and waking up in the same bed, he'd changed toward her. She couldn't quite put her finger on what the look meant, but hadn't Addy used to call it "smitten"?

Nah, it couldn't be. She must be suffering from anemia while she waited for her bone marrow to replenish itself, and wasn't thinking right. Most likely what she saw in Dane's eyes was nothing more than deep gratitude. And before the day was over she'd strike a deal with him. Their relationship would be nothing more than a working one.

After the forty-five-minute hospital visit, Dane took advantage of his mother's offer to continue to watch the kids. They made a quick stop at Rikki's house so she could change, then he took her to a well-known vegetarian restaurant on the Sunset Strip for a late afternoon meal.

"I'm not sure what you need to eat other than red meat to build up your red blood cells, but I trust you know what to do."

She'd changed into a bright pink short jacket that stopped mid-rib cage, and cropped, loose orange cargo pants. She'd put on makeup and had spiked her hair every which way and now it framed her face in a whirlwind. Somehow the total look worked for her. And the bare midriff drove him insane.

Each day he'd spent with Rikki he'd found himself growing more attracted to her unique look. And every moment since seeing her first thing that morning in his bed, he'd fought the powerful urge to kiss her again.

She was the most selfless person he'd ever met, and something from her past had groomed her to be that way. She hadn't opened up to him at the park, like he'd hoped. He suspected she hurt somewhere deep inside, and he wished she'd trust him enough to tell him about it.

She looked delighted that he'd taken her to a place where she fit in, and this time he was the one feeling out of his element.

"You're going to have to tell me what's safe to eat here," he said, leaning in close to her ear and catching a fresh flowery scent. One false move on her part and he'd nuzzle his nose in her neck, not giving a damn what anyone else thought. Come to think of it, on Sunset Strip, no one would give a couple necking a second glance anyway.

She laughed softly, her beautiful brown eyes sparkling in the late afternoon sun, and he couldn't resist kissing her another moment. He leaned in and brushed her lips with his. Zing! Right to the soles of his feet.

She quickly pulled back and he searched to the

very depth of her *café au lait* eyes, seeing an answer he didn't expect. Compared to the woman in her kitchen the other night, the one who'd wanted to jump his bones, she'd changed. "No" was written in her stare, and she looked as regretful as he felt. They lingered in each other's gaze having a silent conversation. She requested understanding, and he made sure she knew he didn't like to be turned down.

A waiter coughed and cleared his throat.

"Will you be needing more time?"

Rikki sat up straight, forcing Dane to lose eye contact. "Oh," she said. "Actually, I know what I want." She ordered a bowl of hearty lentil soup and a spinach salad with fake bacon, and goat's cheese.

Dane picked up the menu and perused it quickly, thinking, *Now that I know exactly what I want, which has nothing to do with food, I can't have it.*

During the meal, Dane's demeanor changed. From the corner of her eye Rikki watched as he gulped down his grilled vegetable sandwich more out of frustration than hunger. She knew he'd wanted to kiss her earlier, and it wasn't fair to keep him guessing about what had changed between them.

"I've been doing some thinking about us," she said.

He stopped in mid-munch and lifted his head. Alfalfa sprouts bunched at the corners of his mouth.

"All my pre-training for the bone-marrow program cautioned about getting involved with the recipient and his family. I know it's too late with our kids, but I think we'd better stop things from going any further between you and me."

He set his sandwich down and wiped his mouth, regret settling in his eyes. "You probably have a point there, but is it that easy? One minute we're hot and heavy, heading for the nearest bedroom, and the next it's all formal?"

"I know it's crazy, but these are special circumstances."

"Can we just turn it off like that? Can you?"

"I'm not sure, but I think it's for the best."

He wiped his hands and mouth. "I want to go on record as being the one willing to get

involved. I think we've got something good to share, but I'll respect your decision. Can't say I like it much, but what am I going to do? You saved my brother's life."

She'd lost her appetite. Apparently he had, too. He motioned for the waiter to bring the check. She sipped some water, hoping to recover her voice. "Thank you for understanding."

He fished for his wallet and threw a wad of dollars on the table. "Fact is, I don't."

They drove in silence to pick up the kids, and as though feeding on the strain between them, Emma, Meg, and Brenden bickered and whined until Emma complained that Meg had hit her.

"No, I didn't," Emma whined.

"Yes, you did," Meg screamed.

Dane hit the steering wheel with his palm. "Knock it off." His voice boomed to the back of the car. The kids fell silent. "This is the stuff I can't handle," he said to Rikki through gritted teeth.

Feeling responsible for the thick tension in the car, Rikki used her favorite ploy with Brenden. Distraction. "I know it's been a long day for everyone. Would you kids like to make mini pizzas when we get home?" Had Dane even planned to take her back to his house? Did they need to stop at the market for supplies first?

With differences suddenly set safely aside, the kids all cheered as one. "Yeah!" Emma and Meg hugged each other.

Dane shook his head and sent her a sideways glance. "What's your secret?"

"Dumb luck."

Rikki opened the bedroom door at her apartment so Dane could carry Brenden to his bed. The twins were spending the night with their grandmother as Dane had to work. It was almost nine and the boy had fallen asleep on the drive home to Rikki's.

The thought of being totally alone with Dane in her house, after their morning encounter, made her knees go weak. Even though she'd made it perfectly clear that they had to keep things platonic, he wasn't taking any part of "no" easily.

Dane took great care to close the door without making a sound. "I'm on call, starting at midnight," he said, taking Rikki's hand and leading her to the living room. He drew her quivering fingers to his mouth and kissed them, sat on the couch and patted for her to join him. "I've got an idea how we can kill some time." There wasn't a hint of teasing in his emerald gaze, and her mouth went dry.

God give her the strength to resist him.

"Rikki?"

"Hmm?"

"I can't run my hands all over your body, the way I want to, because you won't let me." He had the nerve to lift his eyebrow in a most sexy way, testing her resolve. She blinked, but didn't cave in. "I want to know what makes you tick. Why you do all these great things for everyone else, but when it comes to you, you back away. Help me grasp how you can shut down so easily and move on." He stared earnestly into her eyes. "Help me understand you."

"I don't understand myself. How am I supposed to spell it out for you?"

"You can start by telling me what it's like to grow up a foster-kid."

Did he really want to know her? She at least owed the poor, confused man an explanation, but the words just didn't seem to form in her brain. She clasped her fingers and held her fists between her knees. Hunched forward, she ventured a glimpse in Dane's direction.

He sat quietly waiting, eyes steady and trained on her. "Sometimes it helps if someone else opens up first," Dane said. He tried to lighten things up with a huge understanding smile. "And as I love to talk about me, I'll go first." His smile stretched into a full grin. She couldn't help but smile back.

He grew serious. "You know, up until five years ago I had a great life. I graduated with top honors in high school and college, I led both my high school and college football teams to victory, and I only dated homecoming queens. I even married one. I got my MD, finished my residency and went through more training to specialize in orthopedics. Then everything changed." He raised an intriguing brow. "I'll tell you my story if you'll tell me yours."

She relaxed with a sigh. He was giving her a

chance to find out about him so why not take it? As long as she could avoid telling him about her life, she'd go for it. Wasn't distraction the first line of defense? "What happened with the girls and their mother?"

With a do-you-really-want-to-know look, he paused for a beat. "She left. She was even less interested in being a parent than I was. We'd had a nice life together as a childless couple. Lots of friends, travel, parties. Then by accident she got pregnant. With twins! I thought we'd make the best of it. But she resented losing her shape, even though I thought she looked beautiful. She hated being on call twenty-four hours a day. Meg was colicky. Being a mother didn't come naturally to her. And then one day she said she couldn't take it any more, and left. I don't know if she regrets her decision, but I've never looked back. I thought I knew her. But I guess I really didn't."

"Maybe she knew it was for the best?" Wasn't that what *she* had always told herself? *Mom went away because she couldn't take care of me the way I deserved.*

"The girls were only two. Too young to remember her. I don't talk about her to them unless they ask. You don't know how close I've come to telling them she's dead. But someday, when they're grown up, after all the hard part is over, she may decide to come waltzing back into their lives, and I don't want to poison their attitudes about her. I'll let them make their own decisions about her."

He didn't want to bias his daughters against their mother. He didn't sound bitter, but she knew he must hold a grudge. It would be very hard for him to ever trust another woman. "You're an incredible man."

"Hardly. You see how I mess up with the girls."

"You're on a learning curve, that's all."

"Tell me about you, Rikki."

How could she not? He'd just told her things he probably hadn't shared with people outside his family. He deserved to know a little about her. "Let's just say I knew exactly how Brenden felt, being left with a stranger, when all he wanted was his mother and father. But I didn't even have a father that I knew of when I was taken from my mother."

He nodded and leaned closer. Even after the entire day together, she could still smell his spicy aftershave. Tempted to give in to his masculine allure, she withdrew to the safe inner place she'd created early in life to help cope. A place no one else could touch.

"I have such a vague memory of my mother. I remember long brown hair, cold bony hands, like she was skinny or sick or something. I remember the day she left." Her throat tightened, she could barely swallow. Her vision blurred. *I'll be good, Mommy. Please, don't go.* "I remember saying something, protesting, when one of the men picked me up and I watched them take her away. That was the last time I ever saw my mother."

Rikki's eyes brimmed with moisture. She found herself enveloped in warmth and Dane's tight embrace. She curled into his chest and fought back her tears, feeling somehow safe from her past in his arms. "That was the first day I went into foster-care," she said, noticing the scratchy feel and special smell of his flannel shirt. "I was three years old. I lived in fifteen different homes, some for a few months, a couple for a few years. My favorite foster-mother died. After that I was a teenager and I just didn't give a damn any more."

"Oh, sweetheart." Dane kissed the top of her head and rocked her. "I can't begin to fathom all you've been through." He shook his head, like he'd finally realized the truth about her. "You're an incredible person."

She swiped at her tears and attempted to lighten the mood. "Maybe, but I dress weird."

His laugh rumbled in his chest.

"I've never felt like I fit in. Like there's something wrong with me and I don't know how to fix it. Everyone else had families. I was just the extra kid in the house."

"There's nothing wrong with you. You've had rotten luck, that's all."

They sat wrapped in each other's arms. Rikki never wanted to let go. She felt safe and protected. Had anyone ever made her feel like that?

But she'd made a decision to keep their relationship professional. She had to…to survive. Something in her heart knew that Dane was one home she wouldn't be able to casually walk away from, never looking back. And she couldn't bear the thought of being sent away one more time.

After a few moments Dane let up on their hug. "Have you ever wondered about your birth family? I mean, have you ever wanted to find them?"

"I've thought about it, but honestly? I'm afraid of what I might find."

"When Don was eighteen, he decided he wanted to meet his natural parents. It really hurt Mom and Dad, but they helped him search them out. When he finally found out who his mother was, he never went through with actually contacting her."

Rikki studied Dane's fine mouth and lips while he spoke. Was he saying some things were best left behind?

"I think he regrets it."

"What are you getting at?"

"I've been thinking," he said, playing with a lock of her hair. "Before leukemia messed up my brother's life, he was a damn fine police detective. Maybe he could help you locate your family."

"But he's so sick."

"Yeah, but he's got a lot of time on his hands, and having a project he could do over the phone or on the Internet might help his mental attitude while he recovers."

She laid her head back on his chest. "Everyone needs a purpose. You're right."

"So what do you say? Shall I give him the Rikki Johansen missing family case?"

She sighed, a total sucker for his charm. "OK."

Dane got called into the OR almost immediately after midnight. A multiple MVA had brought several severely injured patients to the ER via ambulance. He spent most of the night in surgery, doing an open reduction and internal fixation of both an arm and leg on one of the patients, while another surgeon searched for the source of internal bleeding.

Before he tried to get some rest at 8:00 a.m., he decided to check on his patients in the orthopedic ward. Any excuse to see Rikki again. He needed to make sense out of how he felt about her. Once Don was on the mend, they could pick up where they'd left off.

True, he was looking for a ready-made mother for his kids. True, she went all gooey-eyed around children, especially his daughters. It seemed like the minute she and the twins were together, Rikki slipped into mommy mode. She was perfect for them, and they adored her.

She also hadn't needed more than a few seconds to decide to donate her bone marrow to Don. Only an exceptional person did such a selfless thing—or someone who needed valida-tion. After her history of one foster-home after another, he had a hunch what drove her to make the world a better place.

Special didn't come close to describe Rikki. And her appearance? Sure, it was different than his usual taste in women, but the fact was she turned him on. He couldn't get her petite body and soft skin out of his mind. But how did he *feel* about her? Did he care? *Really* care? Because she deserved that, too.

* * *

Rikki tightened her jaw and answered the call light. Javier had been buzzing every five minutes since she'd come on duty.

"Is it time yet?" he asked, the instant she walked into his room.

A known gang member and suspected drug abuser, he'd been in the hospital for two weeks with multiple fractures from a motorcycle accident. Though making progress with his injuries, his requests for pain shots hadn't waned a bit. Dane had recently increased the intervals and decreased the amount of painkillers to be given. Javier had caught on and was not happy about it.

"We're supposed to be weaning you off the shots and giving you pills. You can either take two pills now or wait another hour for a shot," Rikki said, standing close to his bedside, studying the orders on his medicine sheet.

In a flash he grabbed her arm and yanked her close, causing her to stumble and drop the chart. "I don't want no pills. Get me the damn shot. Now!"

Someone walked into the room and growled.

The next thing Rikki knew, Javier let go of her and got jolted out of the bed by someone in a white coat. It was Dane. He'd practically lifted the patient off the mattress by his hospital gown with his bare hands, heavy casts and all.

"If I ever catch you laying a hand on her again, I'll cut your drugs cold turkey," he seethed through a clenched jaw. "And I'll have you arrested for assault." He shook him several times. "You got that?"

"Hey, Doc, I was just asking about my next shot."

"You're not fooling anyone. As of now, you're off shots. You'll get two pain tablets every four hours, no exceptions." Dane shoved the patient back onto the bed, lifted the chart off the floor, and reached for Rikki's elbow. "You OK?" Adrenaline made his eyes large and dark. They looked wild, like they had when they'd first kissed, only now it was with concern. "Did he hurt you?"

Flustered, but grateful that Dane had stepped into what could have been an ugly situation, she nodded. "I'm fine, thanks."

Walking her out the door and toward the nurses' station, he cupped her elbow and said, "I would have broken both his legs again if he'd hurt you."

CHAPTER SEVEN

Janetta Gleason gazed over the top of her reading glasses. "OK, spill. What's up with you and Dr. Hendricks?"

From the doorway of Janetta's office, Rikki couldn't suppress a grin. "Nothing. We're friends, that's all."

"Every nurse on the ward is talking about how he practically swung in on a vine and saved you from that druggie, Javier."

"I could have handled it. Dr. Hendricks just happened to be in the right place at the right time. Anyone else would have done the same."

"Rubbish." Janetta motioned for Rikki to close the door and take a seat. "Any other doctor would have called Security and let them do the dirty work."

"Then I'm flattered."

"Are you feeling OK after the bone-marrow donation? You look a little pale. That was outstanding of you, by the way."

"I'm still a little tired." It wasn't exactly a lie. The fact that she'd stayed awake into the wee hours thinking about Dane, worrying she was letting the chance of a lifetime slip through her grasp, had left her sleepy that morning.

The marrow donation had her physically dragging, too. It would take four to six weeks for her bone marrow to replenish itself but, all things considered, her hips didn't hurt nearly as much, and she was feeling good.

Who wouldn't be after spending so much time with Dane? And when he'd promised to break her patient's legs again if the guy hurt her, at first she'd been stunned, then had wanted to fly around the room, crowing. Someone gave a damn about her.

Something about the look in Janetta's eyes gave her the distinct impression her supervisor had just read every thought in her mind. Rikki's pleased grin had probably given her away.

"And how are things going with Brenden?"

How could she say enough about the little boy who'd stolen her heart? "He's wonderful. He really seems to be adjusting well to me now. Gosh, I hope to have lots of kids just like him someday."

"Any luck finding his relatives?"

"No. I think they're all in Central America. I don't know what the protocol is in that case."

"Well, things seem to be looking up for you. I'm glad."

"You know? I think coming to Mercy Hospital was the best thing to ever happen to me."

"Great. Then can you work an extra day this week? Cheryl Josephson needs Saturday off."

Between Dane's rescheduled surgeries and overbooked clinic hours, and Rikki's busy life with Brenden and work, they hardly had a chance to see each other over the next few days. The kids, however, saw each other daily at the hospital child-care center. Dane managed to call her a couple of nights just to say hello and see how she was, and she'd called him once to ask how Don was doing, but the shift in their relationship was painfully apparent. And it had been her doing.

Old doubts started to creep back into her mind. She'd blown her chance with Dane.

She'd agreed to work an extra day that week, and on Saturday, for the first time, Brenden resisted going to child care. Six days in a row of pre-school activity were a lot to ask of a four-year old boy. She promised to make up for it on Sunday.

Welcome to the world of single motherhood and foster-parenting. She wondered if Brenden might be better off somewhere else. Still, she took pride in knowing she was making a difference in his life. She had been there for him when he'd lost both of his parents. And she'd be there for him until they found a permanent home for him, though the thought made her heart race and her throat tighten.

She hadn't been back to see Don since her initial visit, but had promised to stop by on her lunch-break today. She'd decided that as they already knew each other, she should be around to offer moral support while they waited for the new bone marrow to take effect. Don having one more person in his corner couldn't hurt.

After rushing through a shared egg salad sandwich with Brenden, she had to bargain with him to leave a few minutes early so she could see Don. Pizza and a video were on her agenda for that night. Considering he'd already begged for a day at the park on Sunday, the boy wasn't doing badly.

Having felt her strength return a bit more each day over the past week, she skipped off the elevator on the second floor to say a quick hello to Don. Down at the end of the hall stood Dane and Hannah Young, laughing and talking more like old friends than colleagues. Hannah kept putting her hand on Dane's arm while they talked, and he kept *not* removing it. Even from this distance she swore his eyes sparkled.

Rikki's stomach went sour. She'd made it clear they could only be friends, and he was already on the prowl. Before Dane had a chance to notice her, she donned the required isolation paraphernalia and slipped into Don's room.

He didn't look any better than before the bone-marrow donation. Maybe even a bit worse? She couldn't tell for sure, but today his skin had a grayish-olive cast to it.

His eyes lit up when he recognized her. "Hey. At first I thought you were one of my nurses."

She smiled and walked closer, trying to hide her ruffled state. "How are you doing?"

"OK, I guess. To be honest, I don't feel very different yet. But Dr. Young assures me it takes a couple of weeks or more for it to take hold."

So Dane trusted Hannah Young with his brother's life.

"Listen, since you're here, I've got some news for you." He reached inside the drawer of the bedside table and withdrew a messy batch of papers. "Dane gave me all your personal details, and I've been making some enquiries. I think I may have news about your birth family in the next couple of days. Have you ever heard of a Colleen Johansen-Baskin?"

Rikki shook her head. The thought of locating her family sent a chill down her spine.

"I'm trying to contact her. I'll let you know what happens."

"Wow, you didn't waste any time."

"I aim to please."

They stared gratefully at each other for a few seconds.

"Are you OK, Rikki?"

"Sure."

"Come on. I'm a cop, I can tell when something's not right."

"I'm upset with your brother, that's all."

"You want me to beat him up for you?"

She laughed.

"Hey, did you know that when I was a kid, I used to purposely tick off bullies just so Dane could save my butt? It used to make him feel needed."

She widened her eyes and giggled.

"He's that kind of guy."

"You mean Mr. Seems-to-have-it-all needs to be needed?"

"Yeah, he used to think I couldn't live without him. The point I'm getting at is sometimes he comes off as overbearing. Just tell him to back off."

No, that wasn't it.

"Other times he comes off as dense. So just tell him exactly what's on your mind."

Well, maybe… How could she explain to Don

that even though she only wanted to be friends with Dane, she didn't want him to be "friends" with anyone else?

Before she could respond, Dane and Hannah entered the room, both wearing isolation gowns and masks.

Hannah hesitated when she saw Rikki. Dane smiled and tugged on Rikki's sleeve when he approached. "Hey."

"Hiya."

"Well, Don," Hannah said, after offering Rikki a cool nod when she'd passed by, "I've got some news for you. Shall I wait until your guest leaves?"

"Nah. Rikki is my blood sister. Go ahead. Shoot."

"After an initial dip, your blood count numbers are picking up. I am cautiously encouraged that the procedure will be a success. We'll know more by this time next week."

"That's great news, Doc. Isn't that great, Rikki?"

"Fantastic."

"I wouldn't expect anything less from such a great source of bone marrow." Dane stood behind her and put both his hands on her shoulders, giving a gentle shake.

Something made her feel as though he wanted to kiss her, and maybe he would have if they'd been alone. Her crazy mixed-up worries about Dane losing interest since they were only going to be friends started to dissipate.

"So, Dane, where are we eating tonight? You owe me one, and I'm calling it in." Hannah's eyes drifted ever so quickly Rikki's way, but danced back to Dane, twinkling and flirtatious.

"Oh. Man, Hannah, I, uh…"

"You've owed me since last month when the Angels beat the Dodgers. Remember our bet? I'm calling it in. Tonight."

"Can we take a rain-check on that?"

"That's what you said last time. Not a chance, big guy. Do you want to sully your reputation around the hospital?"

Why was she doing this now, in front of Don and herself? Hannah obviously wanted to make her stand, and Rikki was damned if she'd give Hannah the satisfaction of knowing how it shook her up. But her lunch-break was up, and she had to leave.

"I've got to get back to work but, Don, it was great to see you. And thank you so much for doing the legwork on that possible lead."

"Hey, Rikki, thanks for stopping by. Don't forget what I said about the other thing. And I'll let you know the minute I find anything out about your relatives." They shook hands, and Don gave her an extra squeeze before letting go. "I'll never be able to thank you enough."

"Just get well. That's all I ask."

Rikki brushed by Dane, who looked perplexed behind his mask but had mumbled "yes" to Hannah's blatant advance. No sooner had they set the boundaries on their "friendship" than right in front of her he'd accepted a date with another woman. Had he no regard for her?

Then she passed Hannah and imagined a smirk beneath the doctor's mask. Some women were horrible.

Self-doubt snuck out of its hiding place and ushered Rikki out the door.

"I'll call you tonight, Rikki," Dane said, surprising her.

"I won't be home," she said, trying to temper the anger in her voice.

At midnight, her phone rang. After the fourth ring, and only because she was afraid Brenden would wake up, Rikki answered.

"Hi," a very-tired sounding Dane said.

"What's up?"

"I've been at the hospital all evening. Don has spiked a temp. He's septic. We've got him on massive amounts of antibiotics, but we've got to watch out for kidney damage. I don't get it—he was doing so well earlier. God, I wish there was something more I could do for him. I feel so helpless."

Immediately forgiving Dane, worry had her sitting up in bed and switching on the bedside light. "Is there anything I can do?"

"No. He seems stable right now. I just wanted to talk to someone—to you. You seemed upset this afternoon, and I wanted to explain about that bet thing. But you ran off so fast I didn't have a chance."

"My lunch-break was over. I had to get back to work. And you could have called me."

"You told me not to." After a pause, he said, "I need you to know Hannah doesn't mean anything to me. She put me on the spot and I couldn't say no. So I bought her a sandwich in the hospital cafeteria. That's all."

Relief, like a cup of cool water, gave Rikki new hope. But, in all honesty, if Dane wanted to date someone it was his prerogative. She'd made it very clear they would only be friends.

"Listen, the girls are with my mom, and I could use some company."

She'd laid the groundwork for friendship. Wasn't that what friends were for, to be there when they were needed?

"I'd really like to see you," he said.

Truth was, she wanted to see him with all her heart, couldn't get him out of her mind for one second, but she didn't want him to think he could just walk all over her whenever he wanted to. That he could change the rules because he didn't like them. Hadn't Don warned her about Dane being overbearing?

Didn't he understand that when she said no, she meant it?

"Well?"

Plus, she had her pride and self-respect to consider… "Yes. I'd like to see you, too." *So much for pride and self-respect, and everything else that made sense in her life.*

Dane tapped on her door within the hour. The moment she opened up, he took her in his arms and smothered her with a kiss. His warm lips and hot breath, combined with the cold night on his coat, gave her chills. She didn't have time to wonder why he had such power over her good sense. All she knew was she was glad to see him. And from the way he felt, he was glad to see her, too.

He pushed the door closed with his back and continued covering her face with kisses. As though she'd been starving for his touch all her life, she welcomed him, kissed him back, matching his desire with her own.

"Damn, I've missed you."

"Me, too." Why did his presence always reduce her to a two-syllable drone?

His hands wandered across her back and over

her hips. Hungry dark green eyes searched her face, neck, and breasts.

He slid out of his jacket. "I need you."

Did he really think she was that easy?

He wrapped her in his arms and pulled her close to his chest, his heat radiating all over her. She looked up and their mouths joined in a fiery caress.

Apparently, she was.

He angled his head to kiss her again, deeper, more forcefully. His hot breath melted her resolve to keep him at a distance. Their tongues met and she tasted Dane's passion, felt it budding in her center.

Every reasonable thought flew out of her head, along with her last whimper of protest. He walked her backwards to the bedroom, lifting her at the halfway mark.

Maybe in the past she'd have been scared of such a big man overpowering her, but not Dane. He may have been large, but he knew how to be gentle. He carried her as if she were delicate china, even as his zealous kiss tested her strength.

He grazed her lips and nibbled as he spoke in a rasping voice. "I know you said we should just be friends, but that's not all I want with you."

She met his gaze and understanding passed between them.

"If you're not sure about this, you better tell me now, because in a few more minutes I can't predict what I'll do."

"I'm definitely not sure about this." She gasped for air and reached for his collar to bring him back to her mouth. "But don't stop," she said, fisting her hands in his shirt before he crushed against her lips.

"What about your hips?" he said over her mouth.

"They're fine," she whispered breathlessly. "Just keep kissing me."

The next few moments were a whirlwind of desire and heat. He placed her gently on the bed, careful not to hurt her back.

He removed his glasses and yanked off his shirt. The vision of his large, muscular chest lightly dusted in tawny hair took what was left of her breath away. He knelt on the bed, passion flaming in his eyes. Her insides turned to warm honey.

She unbuttoned and yanked at her clothes, while he unzipped and pulled off what was left of his. The sight of him in all his naked masculine glory set her heart pounding. Flaring with passion, all she wanted to do was touch him, run her hands across his chest and arms and down to his thighs. His large, thick thighs were made for sprinting and football. She wanted all of him, next to her, on top of her...inside her.

He studied her nakedness with near reverence. The tiniest twitch of his brow and tightening of his jaw assured her he liked what he saw. His huge hand covered her entire breast, yet she felt more than enough for him. She budded and his thumb lingered over her, circling, teasing her, sending chills across her chest and down to her tummy.

He kissed her shoulder, doubling the wave of tingles from her breasts up to her scalp and down her spine. She shivered with excitement under his touch, hopelessly unable to contain her response.

His chest and arms were hard, like marble, his stomach lean and firm. She pulled him down to her, but he stopped her.

"What?"

Before she could protest, he flopped onto his back and pulled her on top of him. "Just in case your hips are still sore."

"Oh." She'd totally forgotten the week-old procedure and the leftover tenderness. "Guess I'll be on top." Somehow, even though stark naked with the man of her dreams, she was able to produce a coy smile.

He grinned up at her.

She straddled his waist and leaned forward to kiss him again, and again, while his hands explored her hips, thighs, and back.

She arched. He took a breast into his mouth, sending chills down to her toes. Then he tasted the other. Her eyes closed to better isolate the sensation. She could barely tolerate the pleasurable waves rolling across her body. She smiled and cooed.

Wanting more, she wrapped her thighs around his tall erection and nearly drove herself mad by gently gliding up and down over the soft, firm skin. A throbbing heat started in her core and grew in intensity until she couldn't stand not having him inside her another instant.

"Did you bring protection?"

He scrambled for his wallet and dutifully produced a condom.

She did the honors of sheathing him and gingerly slid on top until he filled her, sending her nerve endings helter-skelter. She had to move, couldn't help it.

His chest, stomach, and thigh muscles tensed with their lovers' rhythm. She pressed his shoulders to the bed while their hips rose and fell. Warm pleasure burrowed deeper and deeper until she'd taken him all in. She heard a groan, but was so lost in the sensations she couldn't tell if it was hers or his. Their tempo quickened and the liquid heat rapidly turned to flame. She held onto his shoulders, threw her head back, gripped and tightened around him, begging for release.

Their eyes met in primal frenzy—his were wild and dark with passion. She could hardly focus. He guided her hips exactly where he needed them. A perfect place for her, too. He stayed there, working and moving, as long as she needed him, until fireworks launched from her center out to her fingertips and down to her toes.

He let out a guttural growl when he climaxed. The force sent her into more pleasurable spasms, and they moved together until they could breathe again…until they were sated and back in a semblance of control.

"Come here," he said, gathering her snugly to his chest beside him.

She cuddled into his hold and dreamed of feeling this way with him often and regularly. She sighed.

He kissed her ear. "That was fantastic."

She sighed again, this time with pride. She wanted to say, *It's never been this way for me before*, but instead simply said, "Me, too."

His heartbeat lulled her. His breathing subtly lifted and dropped her head. Who cared if nothing made sense? If she'd just made the biggest mistake of her life, letting Dane closer than anyone else in the world? Within minutes she dozed off in the comfort of her friend turned lover's arms.

* * *

The next morning, the phone woke them. Rikki untangled herself from Dane's grasp, and was surprised to hear Don's voice. At 8:00 a.m. he sounded chipper.

"Rikki? I've made contact with that Colleen woman in Pennsylvania."

"Wait, wait. How are you feeling, Don?"

"Oh. Much better. My fever broke last night. Those drugs did wonders."

Dane sat up with an inquisitive stare.

"That's fantastic. May I come to visit you today?"

"I was hoping you would."

"Let me speak to him," Dane said, interrupting and taking the phone.

Rikki's eyes flew open. Did Don know about them?

He didn't give her a chance to protest. "Your fever broke? Fantastic. What did Hannah say?"

Rikki jumped out of bed to get dressed before Brenden had a chance to wake up and find her naked with Dane. She grabbed her clothes and rushed into the bathroom. Dane watched her every move while listening to his brother and answering all his questions. "We've been dating for a few weeks, since before we found out she was your match."

Never in her life had a man looked at her like that. It was a combination of pure sex, fascination, adoration, possession, and entitlement. Well, maybe she was reading a lot into his interested gaze but, whatever it meant, it made Rikki want to ignore good sense and jump right back into bed with him to repeat last night's acrobatics.

He couldn't seem to get enough of her. He'd devoured her inch by inch, sending her out of the sexual stratosphere. And where had that guttural wail come from? Good thing Brenden was a sound sleeper. She'd never dreamed of being ravished by a man before, but Dane, in his hunger and eagerness to please, had shown her how spectacular it could be.

Oh, God. She couldn't let her physical attraction to him interfere with seeing things for what they were. He'd said he needed her. Nothing more. At some point during the night he'd said how great she was with his daughters. He'd even

said she'd saved his brother's life. But not once
had he uttered a word about wanting or loving
her. And since their first date he'd made it perfectly clear how he felt about having more kids.
They weren't compatible, and she must never
forget it.

Was she nothing more than a practical solution
in Dane's chaotic life? Well, that wouldn't do.

Glancing over her shoulder at the handsome,
appreciative and grinning Dane, watching her
every move while he lay naked in her bed, Rikki
had to admit it could get tricky to remember
what she'd just vowed never to forget.

Later that Sunday they'd picked up Emma and
Meg from Dane's mother's house, and had
brought Brenden along, promising them all a
picnic in the park after a stop at the hospital.
Brenden had reminded her she'd given her word
they'd go to the park on Sunday afternoon.

As they all held hands and walked into the
lobby, Rikki couldn't help but think what a
portrait they made.

It was Rikki's turn to call in a favor, and she

had a plan. She let Emma press the elevator button for the fourth floor, promising that Brenden could push it on the way down and Meg could push the "close doors" button going up or down if she wanted to.

When they arrived on the orthopedic ward they marched straight to Janetta's office. She sat engrossed in paperwork, this being her on duty once-a-month weekend.

"Hey," Rikki said.

Janetta glanced up. A surprised look quickly replaced her glare of concentration. "Hi, Rikki. Dane. Kids. What are you doing here on your day off?"

"I'm about to ask you a favor. Can we leave the kids here while we visit Dane's brother in Oncology?"

The grandmother of five looked unfazed. "Sure. Just tie them up and put them over there." She nodded toward the corner of her office with a grin.

The kids giggled.

"You can't tie us up." Brenden made himself the spokesman.

"Oh, OK. Well, then, here." She handed each

of them a pad of paper and some pencils. "You can help me figure out the scheduling."

Rikki smiled, and caught Dane staring at her. Her face flamed, as though she'd just met him for the first time.

"Thanks," Rikki said.

"Be good for Mrs. Gleason, kids," Dane added.

"If you're not back in half an hour, I'm sending out for pizza and you're paying for it," Janetta said with wink and a cheer from the kids. "Oh, and I'll add in a tip for my services, too."

Dane reached for Rikki's hand when they walked toward the elevator. He didn't seem the least bit hesitant to let anyone at the hospital see them together as a couple. She resisted getting too optimistic about what it could mean. After all, she'd already gone back on her promise to herself to keep things platonic. Knowing better than to let her guard down, she'd let Dane into her life. It was probably a huge mistake.

After they gowned up on the oncology ward, Don seemed eager to see them. His coloring was better than the day before, and he seemed to have more energy.

"I feel like a prisoner in here," he said.

"Until we're sure the procedure has been successful, and your labs stabilize, you may as well get used to it. By the way, Mom said she's coming over later for a visit, too."

"Good. I hope she brings some home-made food."

"Well, that's a good sign, if you want to eat."

"Yeah, I'm hungry. A couple of my cop buddies may come by, but they don't like all this isolation business. The least I can do is offer them food."

Don waved for Rikki to come look at his laptop.

"See this? I sent an e-mail last night, and got a response this morning. This woman, Colleen Johansen-Baskin, had a sister who had a kid around the time you were born. She lives in Philadelphia, but said her older sister moved out west and dropped out of touch with the family."

Rikki read the e-mail and her chest quivered. There was a phone number offered by a complete stranger with an invitation to call. She closed her eyes to still her nerves. Did she want to open that door? How much more could she stand to open up?

Dane's warm hands grasped her arms. He pulled her against his chest, and she laid her head back. He kissed her forehead through his mask. "Think it over."

"She could be your aunt. It's amazing how easy it was to track her down," Don said, a proud grin on his face.

He searched for a piece of paper, and scribbled out the number, then handed it to Rikki.

Tears welled in her eyes when she took it. Dane turned her round and cradled her. She'd never had a real family. She'd always been the outsider. Why hadn't they come for her after her mother had been taken away?

She wrapped her arms around Dane's waist and nuzzled her face into the side of his neck, wanting to stay there for ever.

"If Don can find my potential family in only a few short days, why can't they find Brenden's?"

"Good question. I wish I had an answer.

Maybe it has something to do with them not being in this country? Don't forget, sometimes people don't want to be found."

She knew that desire well. How many years had she lived hiding in the shadows? But since she'd met Dane, he'd almost convinced her it was better to be found. Just the thought made her tremble.

A nurse entered the room with the next dose of IV antibiotics for Don.

Dane reminded his brother that his favorite football team had a game on TV that afternoon. Rikki told Don he could call Ms. Baskin for her if he wanted, as she probably wouldn't get around to it any time soon. *Because I don't have the guts to make contact.* After visiting a bit longer, they said their goodbyes and left.

Unsettled with the possibility of finding blood relatives, Rikki withdrew to her safe place—the cave in her heart—and kept Dane at a distance the rest of the day.

On Monday morning, Rikki had just finished changing a dressing on a second-day post-op foot amputation when she was called out of the patient's room.

"You've got a phone call," the ward clerk said.

Rikki took the receiver. "Hello?"

"This is Claire Brodsky from Children's Services. I wanted to notify you that though we haven't been able to locate Brenden Pasqual's blood relatives, we have found another foster-family for him."

The air left Rikki's lungs. She couldn't even form the words to respond.

"They are a Hispanic family with two children around Brenden's age, and the wife is a stay-at-home mom. The situation is ideal and they are eager to take him in for as long as necessary."

Her thoughts swirled around in the sudden dizziness overtaking her. *But I'd keep him for as long as necessary, too.* All she could manage to say was, "How soon?"

"We'd like to pick him up tonight."

She fell into the nearest chair. Her palms went clammy. The room blurred. "Can we wait until the weekend?"

"We feel it would be in the boy's best interests

to move in with the Gomez family as soon as possible. Of course, we appreciate all you have done for him, but you knew you were only keeping him on an emergency temporary basis, and you've had him for almost three months."

Three months wasn't nearly long enough in Rikki's estimation. Knowing better, she'd let him get under her skin and had hoped to keep him permanently.

"If we are unable to locate his relatives and if they don't want him when we do find them, the Gomez family is interested in adopting him."

Her mouth went dry. She swiped at tears dripping down her cheeks and chin. "Is there any way I can apply to adopt him?"

"Well, Ms. Johansen, certainly you can apply, but I'll be honest—little Brenden has a chance to be with a ready-made family and they share his culture and background. It's the best possible circumstances for him, given the situation. I couldn't guarantee your application would be seriously considered as you are single and so young."

"But he's such a great kid. I want him to be in a good home."

"You can trust that we've found an excellent home for him. We here at Children's Services want to thank you for your help, and we will definitely be contacting you again for future short-term foster care. What time would be good to come by tonight?"

Never? Oh, God, she wanted to bolt. She wanted to pack her clothes and run away with Brenden. He'd just gotten used to being with her and now they wanted to upset him again with more strangers. Dear God, what could she do?

"I'll need some time to get his belongings together, and I'd like to have one last dinner with him to say goodbye." Her voice cracked on goodbye.

"Would eight be all right?"

Rikki could barely make it through the rest of her workday. She didn't know who to turn to. Who could possibly understand how she felt?

Janetta? She'd only just gotten her first foster-care ward. She wouldn't understand yet how hard it was to give a child up.

Dane.

He'd seen her eyes light up every time Brenden giggled. He'd been with her the first night Brenden had really opened up. His daughters were the boy's newest best friends. And in her heart she knew Dane, the man who never wanted another child, had a soft spot for him.

On her afternoon break, Rikki snuck off to Dane's office. Fortunately, he was there.

His nurse had just left the room. She and Rikki knew each other from around the hospital. "Something is up," the nurse said. "A month ago he'd have read me the Riot Act for not telling him a patient had cancelled. Today he said, 'No problem.' Can you believe it? Dane Hendricks saying 'no problem'? I'd sure like to know what's going on in his life."

Rikki had seen a change in Dane, too, but she wouldn't let herself think about what it could be from. Certainly she didn't have anything to do with it. Or did she? But today the only thing on her mind was Brenden.

She stood in his doorway. One look at her, and Dane jumped up from his chair and rushed around the desk. "What's wrong?"

The words stuck in her throat. "They're moving Brenden to another foster-home."

Dane wrapped her in his arms and held her close. "Oh, no. Rikki. Honey."

"What am I going to do?"

He didn't offer any solutions. He just stood there and hugged her as close as he could. "Sweetheart. Whatever you need, I'll be there."

In her wildest dreams she wanted to ask Dane to marry her so they could adopt Brenden and be one big happy family, like they'd seemed to be on so many occasions over the last couple of weeks. If only dreams could come true. But her prayers had never been answered when she'd been a child, begging for a real mommy and daddy and family all of her own, so why would things be any different now? And Dane would never consent to more children, let alone a new wife!

"I could use some moral support."

"You've got it."

"Will you have dinner with us and help me say goodbye?"

"Of course. Anything you need."

* * *

"Brenden?" Rikki ruffled his hair, trying her hardest not to cry again. She'd picked him up from day care and treated him to his favorite ice-cream cone, even though it was cold outside and it might spoil his dinner. They'd gone directly home after that, Rikki knowing and dreading what she had to do.

"Yeah, Rikki?" He looked up with his soulful dark eyes from his bedroom door.

She bent down. "Remember when the nice people brought you to me?"

"Yes," he whispered.

"They said I could watch over you until they found a good home for you."

His face twisted in thought. "Are my mommy and daddy alive now?"

"No, honey. But they found a whole new family for you, and they want you to go and live with them."

"Don't you want me any more?"

Her heart shattered. "Of course I want you. I cried when they told me you were moving away." She'd gone through this how many times before with other foster-children? She'd learned her job was to care for them, and then let them go when the time came. She'd prided herself on knowing her job and being good at it. What was different this time?

"I'll be good. I promise."

That was it. Brenden's circumstances reminded her so much of her own. She started crying again and dropped to her knees beside him. Oh, God, she knew exactly how he felt. Her heart ripped in two.

Tears brimmed on Brenden's lashes. One fat teardrop rolled down his cheek. "I don't want to go."

"I don't want you to."

They hugged each other as if they'd disappear if they let go. And sadly in a few more minutes Brenden would disappear from her life. How would she bear it?

"They said I could come and visit you sometimes." Rikki's voice broke so often she had to start the sentence a second time.

"I want my mommy!" The boy dissolved in tears. He dropped to the floor in a puddle, just like the night he'd first arrived. She tried to pick him up, but he was dead weight.

I'll be good, Mommy. Rikki remembered lying in a heap on a cold linoleum floor writhing and crying. *I'll be good, Mommy. Please, don't go.*

But she'd never seen her mother again. And now Brenden was being taken away, too.

Dane held Rikki while she shook and wept in his arms after the Children's Services' representative had bundled Brenden up and left. She cried so hard, he thought she'd melt.

"You don't do this with every kid, do you?"

She shook her head. "Brenden was different."

He couldn't think of one thing to say so he just stood there and held her, offering tissues from time to time. A tight band of anxiety circled his chest; he could hardly breathe. He pinched his eyes closed and rocked her.

When she'd settled down the slightest bit he lifted and carried her to the bed. She curled into a ball. He rinsed a washcloth with cool water, wrung it out, and placed it on her eyes and forehead. He sat next to her and patted her hip.

He'd do anything to take away her pain. The most selfless, giving person he'd ever met didn't deserve to suffer like this. She'd never had anyone to support her, to love her no matter what, to ease her suffering. God, it made him ache inside to think how alone she'd always been.

And now she'd completely withdrawn from him. If he could only chip through to her heart, he could be sure about the new feelings he had for her.

He sat on the bed and gathered her into his arms. Her eyes were tightly closed beneath the washcloth. Her hands were balled into fists. He rubbed her shoulder.

"I get the feeling there is some horrible thing that keeps holding you back in life. Tell me, Rikki. Tell me about your mother. Please?"

She stirred in his embrace. "I can't."

"You've got to tell someone. Share it with me. Come on."

She cleared her throat and lifted the cloth. Her eyes looked distant, focused on somewhere he couldn't begin to see. "I remember being alone a lot. I remember the day my mom left. She told me to go hide in the closet and not make a peep, like a good girl. She would tell me to do that sometimes. I thought it was a game. Sometimes I'd fall asleep, and when I woke up she'd be asleep on the couch. The last time I was in the closet I heard pounding on the front door, men's voices, and my mother sounded scared, so I came out. The big men were leaving with her."

He felt the cords in her neck tighten. He cupped her jaw and gently tilted her face. No amount of tears could wash away the tortured grief he saw.

She bit her lower lip. "I remember saying, 'I'll be good Mommy, please, don't go,' then one of the men picked me up and I watched them take her away." She'd finally let go of her tightly held secret—he could feel her body relax as a flood of tears ran down her cheeks.

He clenched his jaw to fight off the ache in his chest, but couldn't hold back a wave of emotion rooted in love and respect for her. His eyes grew moist, but he blinked away any trace of tears. He needed to stay strong for Rikki. He needed to be there for her, no matter how much it hurt.

"That was the last time I ever saw my mother. And as irrational as it seems, I can't help thinking if I'd only been good and stayed in the closet, maybe things would have been different."

"Oh, God. Honey, what a burden to carry around all your life." His voice was high with pain.

They held each other and she cried several minutes more. For the first time in years he revisited his own grief. When his wife had left, it had been a different kind of hurt, the kind that came with broken trust. He hadn't felt this much raw pain since he'd found out his brother had leukemia. He desperately needed to help Rikki feel better, as much for his own sake as for hers.

Would finding her family help? He cleared the lump in his throat. It was worth a shot.

"Don talked to your aunt this morning. We're positive it's her because she laughs just like you."

She gave a half-hearted laugh, and he was pleased his ploy had worked. She hadn't protested so he'd continue. "She said when your mother died, your grandfather had cancer and your grand-mother was too overwhelmed and couldn't take you in. It wasn't that they didn't want you."

Rikki went completely still. He knew she was listening.

"Colleen, your aunt, was three thousand miles away in college and was too young to help out." He laced his fingers through Rikki's limp hand. "She said it has haunted her all these years, and she'd love to meet you. Your grand-mother died shortly after your grandfather, so your Aunt Colleen and her children are all you have left."

What else could he say? She looked so tiny and fragile, whimpering from time to time. What thoughts were going on inside her head? He longed to erase every bad thing that had ever happened in her life. Had she heard a word he'd said about her aunt?

"Does she know how my mom died?"

"Apparently, no one could stop your mother from using drugs until she overdosed. Sweet-heart, I'm so sorry."

He needed to make her feel better. He wanted

to promise her the world, but knew he might regret it if he promised too much. For the first time since his ex-wife had left, he wanted to trust a woman, to have someone in his life again, someone to share his beautiful daughters with. He wanted to make someone else happy. Whatever it took.

"I thought maybe we could fly out to Pennsylvania and meet her. I'd pay for everything."

"I don't know, Dane, I'll have to think about it. You don't owe me anything, if that's what this is all about."

"I owe you more than you can ever imagine."

Rikki was more than a wonderful person, more than a fantastic lover. He lifted her slack hand, kissed her fingers, felt her waning life force and ached to make her feel better.

She was his friend.

His lover.

He'd fallen in love with her, and he wanted her to know.

Rikki wiped her eyes with the washcloth. She looked at Dane with sorrowful dull brown eyes,

eyes he wanted to make sparkle again. How could he not trust her?

As though she'd read what was on his mind, she whispered, "Just be my friend."

CHAPTER EIGHT

DANE finished his Monday morning hospital rounds and headed for his office. It had been a week since he'd promised to be Rikki's friend. His body ached for hers, but he knew he had to back off, give her time to catch up with him. He'd always been impulsive. Want something? Go after it. Something was wrong? Fix it. His life had been one long list of accomplishments. Check. Check. Check. Until his marriage had fallen apart and his brother had gotten leukemia.

And then he'd met Rikki. He'd found what he'd wanted in a caring person who was good with his daughters. He was lucky enough to be sexually attracted to her, too. It was supposed to be a win-win situation. He'd gone after her without regard to her needs. He hadn't come close to thinking things through, with all the possible consequences.

Maybe it was time for him to broaden his vision to see the whole picture. Since he'd become a father he'd learned life wasn't all about him any more. And now that he'd met Rikki, he understood her needs had to come first.

The last seven days had been the edgiest in his life since waiting to hear if he'd made the cut for medical school. Yet if Rikki only needed a friend, he'd be that for her. She deserved it…and much, much more. If he could just hold out a little longer, maybe she'd start to see the bigger picture, too.

She was going through hell getting over Brenden, not to mention deciding whether or not to meet her only remaining relatives.

He and Rikki saw each other every day, and it was obvious that his daughters loved her. Yet, for her sake, he kept a safe distance.

Dane had a busy clinic waiting for him, and the sooner he got started, the better. He rushed into his office and grabbed the first chart his nurse had left on his desk. A stack of messages begged for his attention, too, but they'd have to wait until later.

He washed his hands and was about to walk

out when Hannah appeared. The somber look on her face made him tense up.

"Do you have a minute?" she asked.

"Of course. Is this about Don?"

"I'm afraid so."

"Let's go back into my office." A sinking feeling made him need to sit down.

"His labs have been plummeting. His white cell count is practically non-existent. Normally, we'd see a rally by now with a successful engraftment." Her voice was strained and she blinked nervously. "If things don't change soon…"

Everything stopped for a moment. The room went quiet, his pulse paused, he didn't breathe—he couldn't. Then, just as quickly, life switched back on. His brother might be dying and he had to deal with it. He pinched the bridge of his nose, squinting hard to help think of some way to fix everything.

"Damn it all to hell."

Don. The kid he'd been insanely jealous of when his parents had first brought him home. His adopted kid brother, the scrawny tag-along who'd driven him nuts in high school, was dying. How many times had he saved him from bullies? His kid brother had been his biggest supporter in his football days, too. Yet Don could never even make the C string.

Was it only the luck of the draw in life for one to be so strong and healthy and the other so susceptible to disease? Don had been a sickly kid, yet had overcome most of his physical challenges. The day he'd become a police officer, after six weeks of grueling academy training, had been the proudest time in his life. He'd taken on a tough job and performed it well and received respect from his peers.

Though Don had always been frail, he'd always made up for his shortcomings with wisdom. Dane had learned to respect the kid who'd bugged the hell out of him. And more than anything, he wanted to know Don until they were both cantankerous old men.

"We could try another bone-marrow transplant," she said.

"No. Don was adamant. Damn. I've got to see him."

"You won't like what you see."

* * *

Somehow Dane had made it through his morning clinic and rushed to his brother's room during lunch. Hannah had been right—what he found shocked him. How could someone change so much for the worse in forty-eight hours? Don looked ancient.

Despite everything modern medicine had done for him, Don looked very sick. Burning up with fever, dehydrated, in pain, ghostly white, he lay listlessly in his bed as if he were a shriveled-up old man. He was only thirty. He'd never have the chance to get married and have kids, or take the trip to Europe he'd always dreamed about, or retire from the police force.

"Hey, brother," Dane said.

Too weak to respond, Don merely nodded at Dane.

"We've been here before. We'll get you through this. You'll pull through."

Dane wasn't sure if he believed what he'd just said, and from the distant look in his brother's eyes, he could tell Don wasn't sure either. Still, he needed to say it for both of them.

"All my papers are in order," Don whispered

in a rasping voice. "They're in the file cabinet in my office."

"Don't talk like that. This is just a temporary setback. You'll pull through."

Don stared at Dane with wise, feverish eyes. Dane couldn't fool him. This was his last chance for a miracle.

Dane offered him a sip of water and prayed the bone-marrow donation would kick in.

"OK, bro," Don said in a weak voice. "It's confession time. You go first."

"What are you talking about?"

"I'll start. I paid Billy Maarschalk off to pretend he was going to kick my butt that time your football team lost to Los Vergennes High School. I thought if you could stop another bully from hurting me it would make you feel better."

"You're lying."

"Nope. Now it's your turn to spill. Tell me about Rikki."

"Honest?"

"If I'm lyin', I'm dyin'." Don gave an ironic laugh.

"She's great with kids."

"You are so full of it, bro."

"Hey, shove it. OK, the truth. I've never met anyone like her, and I can see a future for us. But she insists we should just be friends. What can I do?"

"Leave it up to me."

They exchanged knowing smiles and drifted into silence. Dane sat by Don's bedside for another hour, just to let him know he wasn't alone, until Don fell asleep.

Dane called his nurse and asked her to cancel his afternoon clinic, knowing he'd have hell to pay tomorrow. But he couldn't go on today. Maybe his physician's assistant could see some of the patients who'd already shown up.

Completely drained, all he wanted to do was get away from the hospital. He needed to think everything through. He needed solitude and, thanks to Rikki, he knew exactly where to go.

Janetta called Rikki into her office and gave her the update she'd just heard from the ICU supervisor. If things didn't turn around in the next couple of days, they were starting a last-ditch course of chemo for Don.

Rikki's stomach cramped and she got light-headed when she heard he'd relapsed. She clasped the corner of the desk until her knuckles went white. The bone-marrow donation had failed. She had failed. Don was in grave danger of dying.

Rikki wanted to rush to Don's bedside, but the family had requested no visitors, according to Janetta.

She called Dane's office. She had to speak to him. His nurse told her he'd cancelled his afternoon clinic and left for the day.

The ICU nurses' station said he hadn't been there for a few hours. She called his cell phone, but he didn't answer. Frantic to see him, the minute she got off work she drove to his house. He wasn't home. No one was at his mother's house either.

On a whim, she drove to Fernwood Park. He'd liked it there when she'd shown him her secret thinking cave. She'd thought about going there the day after they'd taken Brenden away, but Dane had kept her busy with his girls. They'd gone back to the spot on several occasions with the kids since she'd first taken him. Maybe he'd go there?

It was worth checking out.

She parked her car, threw on her jacket and scarf, as the early days of December had taken a turn toward colder weather. She strode along the hiking trail, though at four-thirty in the afternoon daylight was already turning to dusk.

She marched up a small hill 'to the crest, winded from the climb. When she stopped to catch her breath, she saw him. Dane sat on a rock in her cave bundled in a coat, stripping the bark off a twig. His face was devoid of expression.

Her heart jumped at the sight. Hurt couldn't begin to describe the distant look on his face. He'd crawled somewhere deep inside and left a "vacant" sign in its place.

"Dane!" she called, and rushed toward him.

He glanced at her but went right back to skinning the twig. Sullen. Withdrawn. Beyond her reach.

What could she say? How could she help him deal with the possibility of losing his brother? She'd never had a brother or sister and couldn't imagine how difficult it must be for Dane. Though she still had vivid memories of losing her mother, and even after twenty-three years, the pain had never stopped.

"Dane, are you all right?" She approached him and held out her hand. He reached for it in a half-hearted manner. His eyes barely made contact with hers. His cold fingers went flaccid in her hand and he let his hand drop from her grasp.

After a few seconds of silence, he broke the twig in half and tossed it on the ground. His face had turned to stone. His eyes were lifeless. He didn't utter a sound.

"Do you need me to watch the girls for you?"

"They're with a friend."

Rikki fumbled to find words, avoiding the helpless feeling that threatened to take over. "There must be one last thing we can try to help Don get better."

"I don't know. All we can do is wait and see how the chemo turns out."

She wanted to cry at the sound of his defeated words. Don was young. Surely he had another trick up his sleeve.

Resting her head on Dane's thigh, she wept. She'd never felt more involved in anyone else's life than with Dane. His pain was her pain. It frightened her.

Dane didn't move, but sat as though he were carved out of granite. She forced herself to stop crying, swiped at her tears and looked Dane in the face. "I'm so sorry."

Several minutes passed without another word. Rikki remembered how as a teenager when she'd come to this cave, needing time to think, she'd wanted nothing more than to be left alone. To never be found again.

She bit her lower lip and searched Dane's eyes. He stared coldly off into the distance. Did he even realize she was there? Maybe her presence reminded him how the bone-marrow transplant had failed. With all hope taken away, maybe he blamed her.

If she could only read his mind.

Rigid and withdrawn as he was, she suspected her presence might bother him. He needed time to himself.

That's how she'd always wanted it to be when

she'd come here. *Leave me alone. I'll tell you when I'm ready to talk*. The way he hardly acknowledged her right now, he probably would just as soon be left alone, too.

She remembered Addy's sage advice. "Timing is everything." Maybe Dane didn't want to be found today, but hopefully tomorrow would be different.

She stood and without another word and all the respect she could offer, she kissed his cheek. He didn't even flinch. She backed out of the cave to give Dane the space he needed.

When he wanted comfort, she'd be there for him. Now was not the time.

Dane watched Rikki leave without saying goodbye. He couldn't bring himself to call out to her. His voice had disappeared after he'd cried and yelled so loudly he'd thought the granite might cave in. Nothing he could do could make his brother recover. All they could do was wait. He'd never felt more helpless or alone in his life.

And Rikki had just walked away. It seemed strangely reminiscent of how his wife had bailed out of their marriage when the going had gotten too tough. Rikki was so busy trying to fill up the gaping hole in her soul by doing things for others that she'd missed the point about healing herself first. She wouldn't be able to love anyone until she did. Well, that was something she'd have to figure out for herself. Right now he had his own healing to deal with.

They were friends. More than friends. He shouldn't have to explain to her how much pain he was in. If she really cared about him, he shouldn't have to stop his grieving to fill her in on all his anger, denial, and self-doubt.

He'd about reached the death and dying bargaining stage when she'd arrived, but his pact with the big guy in the sky hadn't been anything he'd wanted to talk about just then. And how far would he go to save his brother's life? Would he offer his own?

Truth was, the answer was no. There were people and things he wanted to live for.

Damn. Not only was he a coward, he was a failure. And now Rikki had walked away, too, which made him a loser on top of everything else. His thoughts were jumbled and confused. If he could only figure things out. Why couldn't he think straight?

He stood up to run after Rikki, but it was too late. She was long gone.

The last thing he could handle today was history repeating itself. And the one thing he hadn't done when his ex-wife had walked out years ago had been to have a good stiff drink. Considering how this day had gone, he couldn't think of a more appropriate way to end it.

Rikki lay spread-eagle on her bed, staring at the ceiling. She'd cried out all of her tears hours ago and now, emotionally drained and numb to the world, she lay motionless.

Dane didn't want her around. Would he ever want her around again? It had made sense to leave him alone to think things through. How long should she expect to wait for him to call her or come to see her? As difficult as it would be, she'd have to bide her time. For once she'd lobbed the ball into his court, and it was up to him to make the call.

She'd come to her senses and quit blaming herself for the bone-marrow donation not working. She'd done her part, and the rest was in the hands of fate. For some reason the engraftment hadn't been successful, and she'd have to deal with it.

But poor Don. She couldn't give up hope that the chemo would work this time.

Her eyes welled up again when she thought about Don, and what it meant to him. Life and death was the part of nursing she'd never been able to figure out. That was probably why she preferred to be an orthopedic nurse. Broken bones could be fixed, shattered joints could be replaced, but cancer was another story altogether.

She'd thought over her situation with Dane, too. He'd filled up her life with so many wonderful things. She'd grown more confident than she'd ever been since meeting the nitpicking, demanding, and overbearing orthopedic surgeon. He had great kids. She absolutely loved them.

And she loved him.

Dear God, she'd let herself fall in love. The

thought made her want to curl up into a ball and hide.

A sudden rapping on her door pulled her out of her thoughts. More knocking. She sat up. Her heart pounding, she rushed toward the door.

"Dane? Is that you?"

"Yeah. Open up."

Maybe he was ready to talk. Maybe she could console him now. She opened the door with a burst of optimism. His belligerent glare put a quick end to any renewed hope.

Disheveled, he pushed his way into her living room. He smelled of alcohol and seemed a little unsteady.

"I hope you didn't drive yourself over here."

"I took a cab."

He wore the same coat he'd had on at Fernwood Park. His ash-blond hair fell onto his forehead and stuck out at the sides. She wanted to smooth it down, but was afraid to try to touch him. His glasses were smudged and sat crookedly on his nose.

"You know what your problem is?" he said, turning and pointing his finger accusingly at her.

Stunned—suspecting he was drunk—she didn't say a word.

"When it comes to really giving, Ms. Philanthropist." It took him a couple of tries to say it right. "When it comes to giving, you don't have the foggiest idea how," he said with a slight slur.

"What are you talking about?"

"You're so busy trying to help everyone else that you've never fixed yourself."

What? How was she supposed to respond to that? Dazed, she took a step back. How dared he? He'd been sitting in a bar all evening, ruminating over the big questions in life with a bartender, and suddenly he had everything figured out? She didn't deserve to be lectured to by a drunk.

"I won't let you put down my charitable efforts. I think I add something to the world, instead of sucking life out of it like most people."

"Oh, get over yourself. You don't get it, do you?" He straightened his glasses and looked her straight in the eyes. A fruity alcoholic aroma permeated the air. "I needed you today, and you left me. Was it too much just to be there for me? Just because you couldn't cut off your hair, or give me your platelets, it didn't mean there was nothing you could do for me. I needed you to *be there*, but you left."

"I'm not a mind-reader, Dane. You hardly acknowledged me. I assumed you wanted to be alone. I would have wanted to be left alone if I were in your shoes."

"You're just like my ex-wife." He barreled full speed ahead. *"If life gets tough, I'm outta here."*

"That's rubbish, Dane, and you know it. I'm nothing like her."

"Then why did you leave me?"

"I already told you, I thought you wanted to be left alone."

"Wrong answer."

What the hell was he getting at?

He jabbed the air with his finger, widening his belligerent stance. "All the great things you do in the world won't make any difference until you fill that gaping hole in your own heart."

He'd totally withdrawn from her at the park, and now he was drunk, waxing poetic, and forcing his opinions on her. He acted like she'd better listen to his pearls of wisdom or she'd live her life in vain. What kind of pushover did he think she was?

Anger snaked up her spine. She straightened her shoulders.

"You know? A month ago, I might have agreed with you, but that was the old me. And yes, you would have been right back then, but I'm going to surprise you with this next part. I admit it. Knowing you has made me a better person."

Now she'd gotten his attention. He lifted his head, tried to focus his gaze. "Then why don't you trust me?"

She stumbled backwards. Be honest. Put it all out there. He deserves the truth. "I'm afraid."

He stood, his arms akimbo. "Get over it."

"It's not that easy."

"Make up your mind to trust me."

Damn, Don had been right about Dane being overbearing. "How am I supposed to decide to just start trusting?"

He combed his fingers through his hair. "I'm the one whose wife walked out. I should be the one who can't trust. But I know a good thing when I see it. We're good together."

She lowered her voice. "Dane."

"I'm willing to take a risk on us, but you've got to meet me halfway. One day we're close, the next day we're distant. I can't take it. You're so closed off. How can I know for sure I love you, if you won't let me in?"

Her mouth dropped open.

"Make up your mind to trust me, because I'm quite sure I have feelings for you."

Oh, God. She wanted to run for cover. Anxiety thrummed through her body. It was now or never, and she couldn't take the plunge. Tears filled her eyes and she pleaded for understanding. "I'm afraid."

A new expression appeared on his face. Resolve? "Then I can't help you." He tapped his fingertips on his chest. "Don't ever forget you were the one who walked away today."

She couldn't take this. Her hands flew to her ears.

He grabbed her arms, lowered them and stared into her eyes. "I can give you what you need, and you know it."

She couldn't let him be in control one more

second. He deserved to know her reasons for being afraid to love him. She swallowed. "Not true."

"What are you talking about?"

"I'm looking for a man who loves me for impractical reasons. Not because we'd make a great team. I want you to love me because I'm everything you never thought you could love. I want a man who wants kids as much as I do. Not a man who is a decent parent because he feels stuck with two gorgeous daughters who deserve his devotion. Not because those girls need a mother. I don't want a man who doesn't have a clue about what blessings he's got," she said.

He let her go. Perhaps she'd hit below the belt, but he'd been fighting dirty, too, and it was true. She may as well let him know it.

He stepped back. "I know what I've got, and what I want. Ah, hell." He swiped the air with his hand. "This is all too much to handle. My brother may be dying, Rikki. I don't need this added aggravation." He headed for the door.

"My heart breaks for Don, and your family, too. I've tried my best to help out. I'd like to see him, but you aren't allowing visitors outside the family now."

Dane stopped in mid-wobbly step, registering what she'd said. "I'll arrange for you to see him if you'd like," he said quietly.

"Yes. Thank you. And, please, give my love to the girls. You've done a superb job with them."

He pointed a finger at her. "When you come to your senses, you know where to find me."

"Ditto."

So this was how it would be—an emotional stand-off. He walked out the door. She closed it and leaned against it.

Her heart raced in her chest and she didn't think she could breathe. Had she done the right thing, or had she just blown the greatest gift she'd ever been offered?

Right now, too confused to think one more thought about Dane, Don had to come first.

There was another tap on her door. She opened it. Dane looked chagrined. He scratched his jaw.

"I need to call a cab."

She snorted. "No, you don't. I'll drive you home."

CHAPTER NINE

RIKKI and Dane didn't say a single word on the whole fifteen-minute drive to his house. She steered her car with a death clutch from tension, but she was damned if she'd break the ice.

So they'd come to a crossroads and neither could compromise. It was crystal clear they couldn't be together. Finally, they'd *gotten* it.

When she pulled into the high-rise condo driveway, Dane looked like he wanted to say something. He quickly brushed his fingers through his hair, got out without looking at her, but bent back down. "I'll tell the nurses in ICU you have my permission to visit my brother any time you want."

"Thank you," she said, staring straight ahead, determined not to even glance at him.

He closed the door and walked unsteadily toward the lobby entrance.

An urgent need drove her to honk the horn. He turned around, looking confused. She jumped out of the car.

"Could you call the hospital now?" She spoke to him over the hood of the car. "I'd like to see Don tonight."

He nodded, as though, at just before midnight, her request seemed completely rational and normal.

"Thank you." She slipped back into the car, hoping her car hadn't left any oil drippings on the perfectly manicured driveway.

Just past midnight Tuesday morning, Rikki arrived on the Mercy Hospital ICU oncology unit. The lights had been dimmed and, like a barricade, every patient room had a nurse seated behind a desk. Despite the hour, the noise level was no different from the busy day routine. Nurses called across the unit to each other. The ward clerk answered the non-stop phones and called questions to nurses. Orderlies bustled around, delivering equipment or patients on gurneys.

No wonder intensive care patients got so little sleep in the unit.

Rikki found Don's room and started to gown up for the visit. His nurse recognized her as being a fellow nurse at Mercy Hospital. "Dr. Hendricks just called. Go ahead and go inside, though Don hasn't been very responsive tonight."

Her mood sank even further.

They'd changed tack, started more aggressive medical intervention, and hoped his bone marrow would respond. Rikki wanted to cry, but held her emotions inside for Don's sake.

She quietly took the seat beside his bed. Several IVs were attached to ports in his arms and chest. He wore an oxygen mask and seemed to be struggling to breathe. She glanced at the monitor on the wall. His heart rhythm looked normal, though his pulse was too fast. The last blood-pressure reading was as low as hers. He normally ran much higher.

Disillusioned, she touched his hand. He looked flushed and dry, as though he had a fever. When he opened his sunken eyes, they were glassy and deep green—almost the same color as Dane's.

Her heart ached when he recognized her and

gave a forced fearless grin beneath his oxygen mask.

If only things could be different. "I guess I let you down," she said for openers.

He gave a dry swallow. "No. You didn't." The hissing oxygen mask muffled his already weak voice. "You gave me your best shot, and I'll always be grateful to you. Now I'm giving my own marrow a pep talk to go forth and multiply, just like the good book says."

The room went blurry. She squeezed his hand.

"And the only way you'll ever let me down is if you don't call that aunt of yours," he continued.

She gave an ironic chuckle and gave him an I'm-glad-you-don't-ever-give-up look.

"Promise?" he asked, with hopeful eyes.

"OK. I promise." Desperate to find something to do for him, she searched for a lemon-glycerin swab in his bedside supplies, lifted his oxygen mask and quickly wiped his mouth to help moisten his lips. Afterwards, just before she replaced the mask, he smacked his lips like a man who'd taken a huge drink of icy water.

"Thanks."

"No problem."

"No. I mean…thanks for everything." He made a weak attempt to squeeze her hand. "You're my blood sister."

Nothing could stop her now. The tears flowed and she could barely focus on his face, but she smiled and clung to his arm.

They sat quietly for several moments.

"You gonna marry that brother of mine?"

Oh, God, what could she tell him—that they'd just yelled and screamed at each other and would probably never talk again, let alone consider marriage? Never lie to a dying person—her nurse's training took over. "Actually, I think we just broke up."

"Damn. Sometimes he's difficult, Rikki, and I know I told you he was overbearing, but he's a good guy." Don took a great deal of effort to shift onto his side in order to make eye contact with her. "The thing is, I've never seen him look at a woman the way he looks at you. And you look pretty damn speechless around him half the time, too—at least, as far as I can tell. Not that I'm an expert on relationships or anything, but

I'd say you two were a perfect match. You know, in the old polar-opposites-attract kind of way."

More tears. If she could only get past her fear.

"What's the matter with you tonight? You're going all female on me."

Rikki smiled and shook her head. "Your brother. He's such a jerk."

"What has he done now?"

"It's not what he did, but what I couldn't do."

"I'm in the dark here. You've got to give me more."

"He doesn't understand why I'm afraid to take our relationship to the next level."

"Oh. The old 'what if' game."

"What do you mean?"

"*What if* I let my guard down, and it doesn't work out? *What if* we fall in love and get married? *What if? What if* the chemo doesn't work?"

Well, that certainly put things into perspective. She was afraid to let herself fall in love, and Don was dealing with life and death.

"*What ifs* never pay off. If your heart is telling you to love him then listen to it. You can't sit on the sidelines and call it a life. Jump in."

She wished she wasn't wearing a mask so she could kiss him, then figured what the hell, untied it and kissed his forehead anyway.

"*What if* my chemo *does* work?"

"Then I'll be the first one dancing at your welcome-home party."

From where had all the energy come, or, for that matter, the wisdom? He was supposed to be sick and distracted—possibly dying! But he'd detected something Rikki had yet to realize. The look Dane often gave her, the one that brought her to her knees, was something much deeper than a prelude to sex. He did love her in a special way, and everyone else could tell. What an idiot she'd been.

Don had worn himself out with his speech. He repositioned himself on his back and grew very quiet, as if he were in pain. She wished there was something she could do to comfort him. The nurse came in with a gazillion bottles and meds, and she hoped one of them was for pain.

Not giving a damn what the nurse would say, Rikki raised her mask and kissed Don again, hoping it wouldn't be the last time she ever saw him. One of her tears splattered onto his forehead. She wiped it off with her thumb.

"Now, if you'll excuse me," he said, "I've got to visualize my bone marrow multiplying and my white blood cells fighting off any trace of the bad guys. It's chemo time!"

"That sounds like a grand plan."

"Yep. Think positive."

"Mind if I do the same?"

"Mind? I'm depending on it. Now, remember what I said," he whispered, glancing fondly up at her.

She squeezed his hand once more. "I'll never forget."

On Friday afternoon, Rikki had just finished starting an IV on a pre-op patient when Janetta called her into the office. "I just got word from my ICU source that Don Hendricks has undergone a strong rally. He may be in remission."

Rikki fell into a chair and wept with joy. She'd gone by to see him for at least a few minutes each day that week. She'd been careful to time her visits for when Dane wasn't around. Mostly they'd spent the time in silence, but Rikki knew Don appreciated her being there—the way she should have been there for Dane.

"This is so wonderful, I can't believe it. I mean, I thought he was getting his color back and looking stronger, and I hoped, but I was afraid..."

Janetta stood and gave her a businesslike hug. "Never give up praying for miracles."

Rikki wanted to click her heels and run to the ICU, but she had patients to care for. She'd stop by after work and give Don a big hug, but only if Dane wasn't around.

On Sunday afternoon, with Don's constant urging echoing in her ear, Rikki found the piece of paper he'd given her, picked up the phone and dialed.

"Hello? Is this Colleen Baskin?"

"Yes," the voice all the way across the country replied. "Who's this?"

"My name is Rikki, uh, I mean, Rachel. Rachel Johansen. My mother's name was Mara. I think you might be my aunt?"

"Oh, my God. Is it really you?"

Rikki paced her living room as she gave Colleen dates and told her what she knew of her mother. "I went into foster-care when my mother had to do some jail time. I never saw her again, but I do have one snapshot of her." She conjured up in her mind the one photograph of her mother she'd memorized as a child. "Let me see, she had dark brown hair and eyes. She wore her hair long. I used to love it when she smiled at me."

She heard sobs on the other end of the phone. "Mara was a beautiful girl, Rikki. Did you know she was a homecoming queen?"

"No!"

"She had everything going for her, and then she met a slick and dangerous man named Richard Figgen. I suspect he was your father. He took her away from us, made her afraid of everything, got her into drugs, and I hold him responsible for her death."

Rikki's mind spun out of control. Her father had a name? There wasn't one on her birth certificate. How odd that when Rikki had wanted to change her birth name from Rachel, and Addy

Greenspaugh had gone with her to do it legally, she'd chosen the name she'd always wanted— Rikki. She'd thought she was being daring to take on such an unusual name. At fourteen, it had meant everything to her to be different and cool. It had also helped to separate her from her dismal past. She had become her own person that day.

Maybe somewhere in the back of her mind she'd recalled hearing her mother talking to her father, Richard...Ricky? Maybe she'd wanted nothing more than to connect with her father on a deeper level by changing her name.

Her stomach twisted up and she needed to sit down.

"So my mother was an addict?" She bit back her tears.

"Only at the end of her life, Rikki. There's so much more I'd love to tell you about her. She was a great older sister to me. It all changed when she moved out to California, though. He made her afraid of everything."

"If you don't mind, I'd like to keep in touch with you."

"Rikki, honey, I'd love to meet you. I told

that wonderful man Don to tell you to come and visit me."

"Maybe this summer on my vacation?"

"Yes! And in the meantime, give me your e-mail address. I'll scan some pictures and send them to you. I have so many stories to tell you, not just about Mara but about your grandparents, too. You would have loved them."

An hour later, Rikki hung up, feeling connected to a distant yet loving family for the first time in her life. She had an aunt and cousins. She belonged somewhere, with people who looked like her and wanted to know everything about her life.

And she had to admit, after all the years of denying she needed a blood family—because she'd figured out who she was without one—it still felt incredibly good.

Two weeks later, the invitation came. Don telephoned Rikki with new vigor in his voice.

"What's up, blood sister?"

"Don! I heard you'd been discharged from the hospital. How are you?"

"I'm feeling great! Listen, you made me a

promise that when I beat the odds you'd be the first to dance at my homecoming party."

"I remember."

"So bring your dancing shoes this Sunday, two o'clock."

When Rikki arrived on the brisk mid-December afternoon the number of police cars parked around the neighborhood stunned her. As she made her way into Mrs. Hendricks's back yard, the uniformed presence gave a military feel to the party.

Don had touched a lot of lives, and the huge crowd of well-wishers proved it. She knew first-hand how he'd touched hers. He'd pointed her in the direction of her estranged family. But hadn't it been Dane's original idea? He'd put Don on the task to keep him occupied while he'd been recovering. She had Don to thank for getting her in touch with her aunt, and she needed to thank Dane, too. *If* she saw him today, and *if* she had the guts.

Rikki and her aunt had both ended up crying when it had been time to end their phone conversation. Don had helped her make sense out of her mother's addiction and eventual death. Yes, people had free will and sometimes their choices were bad. Sometimes the choices killed them.

Armed with new information, after all the years she'd spent wondering who her father was, she no longer had a burning desire to find out about him. And if her hunch was right about why she had chosen her name, she might consider going back to calling herself Rachel. Maybe.

How many more things could change in her life?

Don had clued Rikki in on how Dane looked at her like no other woman. How could she not have recognized the look of love? One of his glances could send shivers through her body and, more, his look touched her soul. Dane was the special meant-to-be man in her life, and she prayed it wasn't too late to salvage what they'd shared together.

Rikki glanced up in time to see the twins. They broke away from their grandmother's hands and ran toward her, throwing their arms around her waist. Rikki bent down to kiss each of them. "I've missed you, sweeties."

"Why don't you come see us any more?" Meg scolded, with clear eyes and an innocent face.

What could she tell them?

"I'm sorry." She fumbled through a million things to say, but only managed an apology. "I promise to make it up to you."

"I miss you," Emma, the quiet and sensitive twin, said.

Rikki kissed the little girls again. "I've missed you, too." And Dane.

She noticed they wore the bead bracelets she'd made for them out of her special clay the last time they'd spent the afternoon together.

A relative Rikki had never met came to gather up the girls and led them back inside for a group game.

They went willingly and waved goodbye, and Rikki hoped with all her heart she would be able to keep her word about seeing them soon. A twinge of fear threatened to take hold. Her eyes stung and the world went blurry again.

Tears came easily most days now. Rikki couldn't believe she had so much to cry about, but after each crying jag she felt better and more focused. She'd rebelled against her nature for years by stockpiling her sadness. Crying cleansed her and helped her see life more clearly, especially the bit about being a part of Dane's life.

Quickly wiping away her tears before anyone could see them, she found Dane in the crowd. Tall, broad shoulders, strong arms, the handsomest man she'd ever known, he stood a half-head above most of the other men at the party. He held a cup of punch in his hand and was laughing, as if someone had told a really good joke.

They hadn't seen each other since she'd switched to the night shift, and she'd missed him, thought about him day and night, and wondered if she'd passed through his mind from time to time over the last couple of weeks. Had he totally given up on her? She hoped not.

Don was surrounded by well-wishers and wore a surgical mask for protection against germs. She worked her way to the front and gave him a huge hug and kiss. He grabbed her like a long-lost friend.

"Your nose is cold," he said.

"Yeah? Well, put on some music so I can warm up. I believe I owe you a dance?"

They laughed and hugged again, and another batch of guests pushed their way toward the man of the hour. She worried Don might get worn out soon. She backed away, then drifted out of the group.

Her gaze came to rest on Dane, sitting across the yard. Today was the day she'd promised herself to tell him how she felt—no matter how afraid she was.

Dane received a long and drawn-out hug from Hannah Young, and a wave of insecurity almost knocked Rikki off her very high-heeled ankle boots. She caught her balance and stood up straight. Hannah could offer all the sexy hellos she wanted, but Dane belonged with her.

Dane peeled Hannah off and turned to the gaudy, irreverent banner the police officers had brought. *Born to Protect and Serve. Don Hendricks. RIP. NOT!*

Yeah, it was sick cop humor all right, but it made Don laugh, and so it made Dane laugh, too. The thought of how close Don had come to dying still made Dane shake his head. He blinked back the nagging moisture that all too often fogged his vision these days. He lifted his gaze across the lawn. One lone person stood on the other side.

Rikki.

The sight of her made his heart jumpstart. He couldn't help the response. The cloudless bright blue sky with the dependable California sun sparkled through her spiky butterscotch hair. No Mary Jane shoes for her today. She'd outdone herself in party attire, with black high-heeled ankle boots and some sort of baggy high-waisted dress rippling in the breeze around her knees. Her only warmth was from a black velvet bolero-length jacket. She looked great. A faint smile crossed his lips. God, he loved her individuality.

He loved *her*.

He backed away from that thought, remembering how she'd disappointed him. He'd trusted her, and she'd let him down with her pitiful excuse about being afraid. He wouldn't allow history to repeat itself where women were concerned.

Rikki didn't approach him. She hesitated, as though waiting for an invitation. Dane wanted to rush to her and hold her for comfort, but didn't move, just stayed seated. When he'd stared at her for a while she lifted a tentative hand and waved. And when it became apparent to Rikki that he wasn't budging, she walked toward him.

Her high heels kept digging into the grass, making her approach long and awkward. He worried she might twist her ankle or fall. To distract himself, he went back to staring at Don's banner until he heard the sweetest voice he could ever remember.

"Please, don't ask me to leave, because I won't."

Her delicate hand rested on his shoulder, and without thinking he bent his head and rubbed his ear over her cool knuckles. She circled in front of him and sat on an adjacent stool. She smelled like flowers. She reached for and held onto his hand as if she never wanted to let it go. He never wanted her to.

"I could use some fresh air," he said. "What do you say we blow this party?"

She scrunched up her face. "We're outside. It's, like, sixty-five degrees."

"Do you want to or not?"

Some sort of battle went on inside her head for the next few seconds before she gave a mischievous glance. "I'll drive."

He stood and smiled. "Sounds like a plan." He took her hand and walked her to her clunker. They got inside, not saying a word. She started it up, needing three tries to get the engine to turn over, and drove up the street. He sent her a silent message.

She slanted him a sideways glance, as though she'd read his mind, made a screwball turn to get on the right freeway, and with a little extra adrenaline in his system, they headed in the direction of his condo.

He wasn't sure what would happen once they got there. He really didn't want to argue any more. Though he knew one thing for certain: he didn't want to spend any more time without Rikki. Evidently Rikki was on the same wavelength. She parked the car in one of the visitor spots and got out.

"I'm going to fix you a cup of that tea you like so much," she said matter-of-factly.

He gave a noncommittal nod. "Fair enough."

Again, they didn't say two words in the elevator, but he had to admit that having her near made him feel alive again. He unlocked his door, and she breezed by and straight into the kitchen, as though she lived there. He leaned against the wall in silence and watched her refamiliarize herself with his cabinets. He kept his hands where they'd be safe, in his pockets, while she filled the teapot. He couldn't trust that he might want to touch the wisp of hair on her neck, or circle her perfectly shaped ear with the silver piercing with his fingertips, or turn her face so he could stare into her huge brown eyes until he needed to kiss her while she waited for the water to boil.

No. He'd stay right where he was, stoic and withdrawn.

Rikki had never been more flustered in her life. Completely unsure if Dane wanted her there or not, she went about her business. Even if he didn't want her around, she longed to be near him and, yes, she did love him.

The realization made her fingers clumsy and she ripped a teabag and had to throw it away. She loved him with all her heart and, no matter how hard she tried to deny it, she couldn't help but love him. He'd have to throw her out of his condo in order to get her to leave today.

Something made her glance over her shoulder. She tried not to come undone at Dane's penetrating gaze. She'd seen that look before, and it usually had nothing to do with asking her to leave. The fine hairs on her neck and arms prickled. How did he manage to have such power over her?

She couldn't hide the small tremor in her hand

when she gave him a clanking cup and saucer. He smiled appreciatively when he took it. No. There was far more than appreciation in his gaze. She had to turn away before she got her hopes up. She picked up her own cup and gave a quiet sigh. She needed to gather her composure, or before long she'd burst.

He took off his jacket, kicked off his shoes and sat on the couch. She sat at the opposite end, and they drank their tea in strained silence. She followed his lead and unzipped her boots, removed them and wiggled her toes. Who'd decided that ultra-pointy shoes should be in style anyway?

She drank more tea then placed her cup on the end table and ventured a look at Dane. He sat, staring at his cup. With sudden conviction she needed him to know how she felt about him.

"I've really missed you and the girls. It felt like a whole part of my life had disappeared after our argument."

He looked up, expressionless.

"The fact is, I didn't realize what I was feeling because I'd never felt it before I met you." She attempted to swallow something the size of a dry sock, realizing it was time to *show*, not tell.

She scooted over to him, removed the teacup from his grasp and placed it on the table. She took him into her arms and drew his face to hers, his warm breath caressing her skin. He didn't resist. With every ounce of compassion and love she felt for Dane, she kissed him gently. He came to life after the kiss, pulled back and gazed longingly into her eyes.

"I've missed you more than you'll ever know," she whispered, and pressed her lips to his again.

Apparently at a loss for words, he drew her closer and kissed with purpose—a hungry kiss that made Rikki's heart race. Over and over they made love with their mouths. Fiery kisses that burned a path to her very center drove her to lie back on the couch and pull Dane with her. He dove into her neck with more hot kisses, and she wove her fingers into his hair in a futile attempt to control her response. She inhaled his clean scent and savored each and every touch of his lips.

"Before this goes any further," she said, breathlessly, "you need to know one thing."

He lifted his head and looked at her with un-focused, hooded eyes.

"What if I told you that I love you?"

"I might tell you the same thing back."

"Well, I just hope you realize that I'm the most worthy person you'll ever meet to love."

For the first time that day, Dane smiled. "You want to know what I've been thinking?"

"I'm almost afraid to ask, but what?"

"You *are* the damn most worthy person I'll ever love."

She caught her breath from sheer joy. They'd finally told each other. She pulled his face to hers and captured his smiling mouth with her own. His tongue welcomed her and they danced through several more minutes of steamy kisses until she wanted more than anything in the world to be naked with him.

CHAPTER TEN

"WHY do you always insist on carrying me in here?" Rikki asked, nuzzling her head into Dane's neck, thrilled down to her toes to be swept away by his strong arms and warm chest.

"Because you're so cute and liftable."

"Liftable? Is that even a word?" She giggled and snorted, embarrassing herself.

"Yeah, it's a word. I created it just for you. Liftable makes me feel…uh… Damn horny is what it makes me feel." He carried her down the hall and into his bedroom.

After yanking back the bedspread, he gently placed Rikki in the center of his bed and proceeded to unbutton and remove her dress. She kept perfectly still and, mesmerized by his attention, stared at the passion in his eyes—quickly getting lost. She co-operated when he lifted the dress over her head, and felt a tickling in her belly when he unhooked her bra.

Her breathing quickened at his reverent gaze. The look abruptly changed to hunger and need, sending a shiver to her core.

Dane peeled down her stockings then swept his hands up her thighs until he reached her lace underwear. She tightened her muscles in anticipation. The breath caught in her throat when Dane drew out the moment by running his palm across her stomach, and down, grazing her mound. Heat flicked between her legs when she shimmied to assist him with removing the garment. Yeah, she'd made the right choice in panties today.

The desire in his eyes alone made her want him, but his touch turned her longing to need.

She didn't speak, not wanting to spoil the moment.

Dane rose up on his knees and unbuttoned his shirt, then pulled his undershirt over his head as quickly as humanly possible. The sight of his broad shoulders and muscular chest dusted with tawny hair made blood rush to the surface of her skin. Warm and willing, she watched as he undid his belt and removed his slacks and briefs, releasing himself.

The man was gorgeous, but what excited Rikki even more was that he wanted her. And she'd missed being with him. Nothing had ever been like it.

The need in his dark green gaze kept her spellbound when he hovered over her on his hands and knees. Would she ever grow tired of staring into those eyes? The intensity frightened her as she outlined his chest, shoulders, and arms with her palms.

After a hungry smile crossed his lips, he swallowed. "You're so beautiful."

She couldn't bear being apart another instant and reached for him. He welcomed her into his tight embrace. Now skin to skin, she reeled with sensations at every point of contact. She inhaled his masculine scent and felt his erection on her thigh, then pressed into it.

They clung together, kissing and rolling around on the bed for several minutes. His hands explored every part of her, tickling, brushing, grazing, kneading—hungry to touch her more deeply. And she let him.

Swept up by his touch, she wrapped her legs around his waist, pulled him closer, and he entered her, rocked and withdrew. She savored his exquisite, slick feel and opened to bring him deeper, then tightened to hold him in place. She let him withdraw and moved to bring him back.

Ready. Wet. Nerve endings on fire. Deeply in love. Deep inside. They didn't bother with protection. They belonged together, like this. For ever.

Their tongues and lips tangled, nonstop. His warm palms traced a trail over her tightened breasts. She moaned with pleasure when he lifted and cupped all of her. He tested her pebbled nipples first with his thumb, then his tongue. She arched and he drew her into his mouth as his hips drove deeper inside her. On and on they grappled and lunged, heightening their sensations…their need.

Later, amidst wild breathing and restless desire, when she didn't think she could bear another second of pleasure, he brought her to the brink. She coiled tighter than she could ever remember. Dane made several quick thrusts, and she strained against him, higher and higher, before shuddering her release. The world broke loose, and she descended into a freefall of sensations.

He slowed down…and stopped.

"I love to feel that. To know I brought you all the way."

So wrung out, Rikki couldn't respond. She groaned her continued pleasure. He laughed and growled back at her. And when her spasms calmed down, he moved deeper inside, as though determined to keep her with him. He worked her quickly back to frenzy and, fisting the sheets in her hands, she came again. He felt like steel and she took him as deeply as she possibly could, until he pumped liquid heat into her.

They collapsed in sated bliss, staying as close as possible. And Rikki knew without a doubt that this was where she belonged for the rest of her life.

A few minutes later Dane stirred from his contented trance. He searched for and kissed Rikki's fingers. He stared into her huge, dreamy eyes. He knew what he had to do, and there was no time like the present.

He nervously nibbled and sucked on her fingertips. "I only thought I'd been in love before, until I met you. You came out of nowhere one day at the hospital, and I thought, Wow, who is that woman? I felt our chemistry immediately."

Her eyes were huge with amazement.

"You surprise me. You make me laugh. I adore your crazy get-ups and spiky hair." He tugged on a tuft of it.

She shook his hand off as if he were a pestering brother. "Stop it. Go on."

"You've taught me how to care about people besides my immediate family. Damn, I can't tell you how much you've added to my life."

Big tears filled her eyes; her lips trembled with expectation. "You're doing great. Go on."

"You want more?" He wanted to please her, to make her understand how much he loved her. He remembered the phrase she'd said she needed to hear the night they'd broken up, and repeated it. "I love you because you're everything I never thought I could love. With all my heart, I *want* you to be my wife more than anything else in life. I *want* you to be mother to my daughters." He dove into her eyes, searching for her soul…her honest answer. "I *need* you to love me, and I *want* you to be the mother of all my future children. So, what do you say? Will you marry me?"

Without hesitation, Rikki squealed, "Yes! Yes!"

He laughed before he grabbed her and smothered her mouth with his.

They settled down, Dane realizing the momentous significance of what he'd just asked. His life would never be the same. He was ready for it. Hell, it had changed the day he'd followed a scrawny, frustrating nurse out to her car in the Mercy Hospital parking lot and asked her out for dinner.

They lay silently in each other's arms for several seconds, deep in thought.

Rikki was shocked that Dane's proposal had included children. "What changed your mind about having more kids?"

"You."

She smiled reassuringly. "You're a good father."

He laced his fingers through hers and kissed her knuckles.

"You know?" he said.

"Hmm?"

"Don will be very happy about us getting married."

"I know," she said. It occurred to her that she hadn't told Dane about her aunt. That even though Don had tracked her down, she'd never thanked the person who'd instigated finding her in the first place. "And by the way, I believe I owe you thanks."

"Well, I know I'm great in bed, but there's no need…"

"Oh, get over yourself." She playfully slapped his arm. "Besides, it takes two to make great love." She rose up onto one elbow, facing him. "No, what I'm saying is I need to thank you for putting Don on the task of finding my family. It was your idea."

He lifted his brows in understanding.

"I've talked to my Aunt Colleen on the phone, and even though I haven't met her yet, I feel like I have a real family now."

Looking more than pleased with himself, he kissed her arm.

"You're welcome. And soon I hope you'll feel like you have a real family with me and the girls, too."

Her heart clutched at his statement. "I already do." God, she loved him. Their eyes connected. Gratitude. Understanding. Love passed between them.

And before long, they were ready to make love again.

After a brief nap, they woke up hungry. Rikki wrapped herself in one of Dane's sweatshirts, put on some of his socks, and drifted toward the kitchen. She'd plopped her purse on the table and her cell phone had fallen out. The red missed-call light blinked. She'd left it on vibrate for the party. She decided to check her messages.

It was from Children's Services, and they asked her to return the call.

She quickly dialed their number, excitement whirling through her. Would Brenden be coming back?

"Yes, Ms. Johansen, I'm glad you called. We have a fourteen-month-old baby in need of emergency shelter. Are you available?"

Dane wandered into the living room, searching for his shoes.

"Can you hold on a moment, please?" Rikki covered the phone speaker. "Dane! They want me to take in another child."

Dane knew this was a defining moment. He'd just told her he loved her and wanted to marry her. It had been a full disclosure proposal. She'd always be taking in foster-children, like other people took in stray cats. He knew Rikki's dreams of having a big family, too. Hell, they hadn't used birth control all afternoon. He understood what he was getting into.

No need for conversation. He gave an encouraging nod. She almost jumped up and down when she told the person on the other end of the phone she'd be available within the hour.

While Rikki quickly showered and dressed, Dane called his mother and explained why he wouldn't be coming back to the party. With loud conversation and chatter in the background, obviously still surrounded by family and friends, she agreed to keep the twins for the night and assured him she understood.

Don broke into the conversation. "You'd better have a good reason for bailing on my party, bro."

"The best, brother. I just asked Rikki to marry me."

Dane had to hold the phone away from his ear for the loud catcall Don made. If he hadn't been sure about Don being on the mend before, he knew now.

When Don settled down he spoke in a raspy voice. "Pencil me in as best man."

Dane smiled into the phone.

They drove to Rikki's house, where she rushed to make the guest room suitable for the toddler. He offered to help her attach a bedside rail on the child's bed while she placed colorful stuffed toys along the wall. She rushed around putting in electrical socket protectors while he put clamps on the handles of every single lower cupboard and cabinet. It brought back memories of when his daughters had been younger. Now he had a new love and a future wife, and he'd do whatever it took to make Rikki happy.

"So tell me about her," he said.

"All I know is she's fourteen months old, and her name is Lily Chow."

No sooner had she said that than the doorbell rang. He followed her to the other room. The same woman he remembered from when they'd taken Brenden away stood on the other side of the screen with a small bundle in her arms.

"Won't you come in?" Rikki swept open the door and the woman entered with a beautiful little girl in a white hooded windbreaker, matching coveralls and shoes with bunnies on them.

Dane's heart pinched at the sight. A beautiful, helpless child needed shelter, and Rikki wanted nothing more than to help her. Truth be told, so did he.

"This will only be a temporary stay, two to three weeks. Her father was arrested for spousal battery. The mother is in the hospital and he's going to jail. No immediate relatives in Los Angeles beyond an uncle who's a known drug dealer. Until Mrs. Chow can get back on her feet, Lily here needs shelter."

Damn, did the child understand what was going on?

Rikki grinned a heart-melting smile, and reached for the little girl. "May I?" she asked the woman.

Lily's black eyes widened, but she didn't protest...at first. Once the transfer had been made into Rikki's arms, the little girl looked back at the Children's Services representative. Then she wailed.

Rikki bounced and patted, walked and sang to the child to calm her down. It didn't help. But she seemed less flustered than when she had first been faced with Brenden.

The representative handed Dane a suitcase. "Are you living here?"

"Me? No. I'm just here for moral support."

"Well, if you intend to spend the night in this household, we need to do a background check for our records. Maybe you should consider taking the training classes and apply for a license."

"He's a doctor," Rikki broke in over the crying child's racket.

"I'm an orthopedic surgeon at Mercy Hospital."

"That doesn't make you any more qualified to be a foster-care provider than anyone else," the woman said with a flinty glance.

He scratched his jaw. "If you have the paperwork I need with you, why don't you give it to me now?"

Had he ever in his entire adult life expected to hear those words coming from his mouth? And, more importantly, had he ever seen Rikki look more surprised and happy? His proposal hadn't even drawn that kind of response.

Dane held the squirming Lily while Rikki signed all the necessary documents for the transfer of the child to foster care. The representative handed Dane a packet of forms for him to fill out at his leisure and, bidding them both good night, she prepared to leave.

"I'll be in touch in the next few days with an update on Mrs. Chow's condition. In the meantime, take care, and thank you," the woman said, one foot already out the door.

When they were alone again, Dane and Rikki looked at each other expectantly. Lily stopped fidgeting long enough to realize the woman had left, and went back to fussing. A few inconsolable minutes later Dane thought an alien force had inhabited him when he heard himself say, "Here. Let me take her."

Having not made any progress in consoling the child, frustration in Rikki's eyes, she gladly handed Lily to Dane. He was right. She did need a break.

He took the wailing child into his arms and placed her on his shoulder. "This used to work with Meg and Emma when they were teething." He rubbed Lily's back, patted her bottom, paced the living room, and started to sing Hush Little Baby.

Rikki's jaw dropped. She stared at him as though in awe. "Both my girls were colicky," he explained.

He'd learned a few things over his years as a parent. And who knew how many more children he'd wind up with? Loving Rikki meant having a big family, sharing his home with foster-children, and maybe a few more of his own?

For the first time in his life he felt ready for it. And when he glanced at Rikki's beaming face, the rewarding look of love only proved his point.

He rubbed Lily's back and patted her bottom, bouncing her up and down with each step. He drew a hushed breath when she settled down, and he continued to sing. Happier than he could remember, he smiled at the woman he loved, and she smiled back. He sent a special message through the lullaby, followed by a wink. "Daddy's gonna buy you a diamond ring."

EPILOGUE

FOUR months later…

Rikki followed Dane into the donor center. It had been a few months since he'd last donated platelets. She had decided to keep him company as he'd been in surgery all day, and she'd hardly had a chance to see him the previous day. Her shift had ended at four, and she'd had a doctor's appointment after that. They'd met up in his office and walked downstairs together.

"Hey, Dr. Hendricks," Sheila, the donor center nurse, greeted him. "Have a seat right here." She glanced at Rikki. "You won't be donating, right, Mrs. Hendricks?"

Rikki shook her head, wondering if she'd ever get used to hearing those incredible words. *Mrs. Hendricks.* "Not for a while."

"What's new, Sheila?" Dane asked, sitting down.

"Same old, same old. How about you?"

"Today was arthroscopy day," he said, loosening his tie. "Four knees and two shoulders."

"Sounds exciting."

The nurse walked off to gather her equipment while Dane rolled up his sleeves. He leaned over the chair to give Rikki a kiss. She closed her eyes and welcomed him. Would she ever grow tired of kissing her husband?

"How did the ultrasound go?" he asked. "I'm really sorry I couldn't get out of surgery to be there."

"That's OK," she said, patting his arm. "The ultrasound tech thinks he might be a boy."

"Our kid was giving the male salute?"

She giggled. "Well, not exactly, but enough to make the tech think *it* is a *he*."

Dane grinned and leaned back when Sheila reappeared to start his IV. "Did you hear that, Sheila? We may be having a boy."

She smiled at both of them. "You two work fast."

Rikki felt a blush come over her—they'd only been married three months. Dane made a big deal out of patting her thigh. "Yep," he said, with a wink. "Now, hit me with your best shot."

Rikki snuggled back into the adjacent chair and held his free hand while Sheila prepared to insert the intravenous line. Nervous for him, she twiddled with her hair. She'd been growing it out again so she could donate to Care to Share Your Hair again. Growing like crazy with the extra hormones of pregnancy, it had already reached mid-neck.

"I've been thinking. If we have a boy, I want to name him Don."

"That's great, but these tests aren't one hundred percent sure, you know," Dane said with a grimace when the needle pierced his skin. "'Tis but a flesh wound," he blurted out, his knee-jerk response.

She snorted. Would she ever grow tired of his corny sense of humor? She settled back on her chair while Sheila taped him up. "I just know it's going to be a boy. I'm positive."

"Well, it's always best to have a back-up plan, you know, in case things don't turn out as you expect."

"OK." She crossed her arms and legs and pumped her foot, while thinking.

After a few moments of silence Dane asked. "So, what do you suggest we name the baby if she's a girl?"

She tapped her finger on her lip and stared up at the ceiling. She lifted a brow and gave Dane a coy glance. "I have a great idea."

"Well?"

Rikki reached over and kissed him between the eyes. "How about we call her Don?" She grinned, totally pleased with herself, and kissed him again.

He looked confused, as though he thought she might have lost her mind.

"D-A-W-N. Dawn."

MEDICAL™

Large Print

Titles for the next six months…

August

THE DOCTOR'S BRIDE BY SUNRISE	Josie Metcalfe
FOUND: A FATHER FOR HER CHILD	Amy Andrews
A SINGLE DAD AT HEATHERMERE	Abigail Gordon
HER VERY SPECIAL BABY	Lucy Clark
THE HEART SURGEON'S SECRET SON	Janice Lynn
THE SHEIKH SURGEON'S PROPOSAL	Olivia Gates

September

THE SURGEON'S FATHERHOOD SURPRISE	Jennifer Taylor
THE ITALIAN SURGEON CLAIMS HIS BRIDE	Alison Roberts
DESERT DOCTOR, SECRET SHEIKH	Meredith Webber
A WEDDING IN WARRAGURRA	Fiona Lowe
THE FIREFIGHTER AND THE SINGLE MUM	Laura Iding
THE NURSE'S LITTLE MIRACLE	Molly Evans

October

THE DOCTOR'S ROYAL LOVE-CHILD	Kate Hardy
HIS ISLAND BRIDE	Marion Lennox
A CONSULTANT BEYOND COMPARE	Joanna Neil
THE SURGEON BOSS'S BRIDE	Melanie Milburne
A WIFE WORTH WAITING FOR	Maggie Kingsley
DESERT PRINCE, EXPECTANT MOTHER	Olivia Gates

MILLS & BOON®
Pure reading pleasure™

0708 LP 2P P1 Medical

MEDICAL™

Large Print

November

NURSE BRIDE, BAYSIDE WEDDING	Gill Sanderson
BILLIONAIRE DOCTOR, ORDINARY NURSE	Carol Marinelli
THE SHEIKH SURGEON'S BABY	Meredith Webber
THE OUTBACK DOCTOR'S SURPRISE BRIDE	Amy Andrews
A WEDDING AT LIMESTONE COAST	Lucy Clark
THE DOCTOR'S MEANT-TO-BE MARRIAGE	Janice Lynn

December

SINGLE DAD SEEKS A WIFE	Melanie Milburne
HER FOUR-YEAR BABY SECRET	Alison Roberts
COUNTRY DOCTOR, SPRING BRIDE	Abigail Gordon
MARRYING THE RUNAWAY BRIDE	Jennifer Taylor
THE MIDWIFE'S BABY	Fiona McArthur
THE FATHERHOOD MIRACLE	Margaret Barker

January

VIRGIN MIDWIFE, PLAYBOY DOCTOR	Margaret McDonagh
THE REBEL DOCTOR'S BRIDE	Sarah Morgan
THE SURGEON'S SECRET BABY WISH	Laura Iding
PROPOSING TO THE CHILDREN'S DOCTOR	Joanna Neil
EMERGENCY: WIFE NEEDED	Emily Forbes
ITALIAN DOCTOR, FULL-TIME FATHER	Dianne Drake

MILLS & BOON®
Pure reading pleasure™

0708 LP 2P P2 Medical